THE CORPSE IN THE CAB

by Aldin Vinton

WILDSIDE PRESS

CHAPTER 1

THE snow drifted like gray feathers in the dark, moist air, but it stung my cheeks and melted sloppily under my feet, as I plodded along the empty streets, cursing this business of living in the suburbs. I was late that night, for I had gone with some of the boys from the press room to pass judgment on a new drink that George Cobb had invented and which had met with such approval that I missed the last express on the "L" and had had to ride home on a local.

The clock in the hall was just striking two as I let myself into the apartment. The embers, still faintly pink on the hearth, gave off a pungent warmth and the room was so inviting after the damp chill of the street that I flung off my wet things, slipped into the dressing gown and slippers that were always laid out for me and settled into my favorite armchair for a final cigarette before turning in.

I was jolted from a delicious, drowsy haze by a ringing of the bell—a long, uncertain jangle as if someone were pushing the button with an importunate but unsteady finger. I muttered something under my breath which would have shocked my little mother if she had been awake to hear it and stumbled to the speaking tube.

"Hello, who's there?" I called.

"I'm sorry to disturb you, mister, but, you see, I—ah—well . . ." The voice in the tube died away into a nervous cough.

"Who are you and what do you want?" I demanded impatiently.

"Well, you see, mister, it's like this," the voice began again. "I got a taxi outside and there's a gentleman in it what gave me this address, but he don't seem able to come in. If you could just step outside a minute and give me a hand maybe—"

I clicked the lid back on the speaking tube with some irritation. Had one of my companions of the evening got so tight he was afraid to go home to his wife and had he come way out here to bunk with me? I could think of no other explanation for a caller at this hour, especially one who was unable to get out of the cab without assistance. Glad that I only had a mother and not a wife to demand explanations, I went out to lend a hand.

In the apartment vestibule a bedraggled, stocky little man was nervously scanning the names on the letter boxes. He looked up quickly as I opened the door.

"Good evenin'," he muttered and pulled unhappily at his damp, drooping mustaches.

"It's nearer morning and not a very good one," I responded ungraciously. "Now what is all this about? Is this man still out in your cab?"

"Sure, he's there and I can't get him to come in. I'd like to be

3

gettin' along. This isn't my beat anyway, and I'm supposed to go off at one o'clock."

I saw through the glass of the outside door that the snow was no longer falling, but the walk was still covered with wet flakes.

"I don't like to go out in my house slippers," I said. "You bring him to the door and I'll get him up the stairs."

"I'd rather you'd come out, too," muttered the man.

"What is the matter with him, anyway? Did he ask for me, are you sure?"

"Well, no, he didn't rightly ask for you. He gave me this address and when we got here, he couldn't get out of the cab. I didn't know which apartment he was coming to, and yours was the only one that had a light still burning, so I thought—"

"So that's how it is!" I interrupted, as the man hesitated and fumbled with his cap. The incapacitated passenger must be Mr. Merton. He was the only tenant in the building who was at all likely to be coming home at this hour in too sad a condition to get out of the cab. He was a heavy man and lived on the third floor; the cabby would need help to get him home.

"Lead on, Macduff," I said resignedly. I stepped out gingerly into the wet snow. The cab stood at the curb, looming dark in the white, deserted street. Its door was ajar, and as I swung it wide, I saw, huddled grotesquely in one corner of the cab, the relaxed figure of a man in a black overcoat. I saw at once that this was not Mr. Merton; this man was much smaller and thinner than my rotund neighbor. His face was half hidden by his black derby which had tipped forward, balanced on the long thin nose of its wearer.

I was seized with a sudden feeling of dread. I nerved myself to reach in and lift the hat from the man's face, and then drew back with an instinctive gesture of horror. The man stared up at me with a livid, sightless gaze. His face was ghastly white and his mouth twisted into a painful grimace. I ripped a glove from one of his limp hands and found it cold and pulseless.

"My God, I think he's dead!"

"I was afraid of that," muttered the cabby in a weak and mournful voice, but proffered no further explanation.

"Who is this man and how did he get into your cab?"

"I dunno who he is, mister. I never drove him before—not to know it. He got in the cab hisself, by the Congress Hotel. This is the address he said and I drove him here. Took an hour nearly, 'cause it's slippery going. That's all I know about it, mister, honest it is."

"Well, I've never seen him before, I'm sure, and he couldn't have been coming to my apartment. However, he may not be dead; only fainted or something. We'd better carry him in and call a doctor. Come on, you take his feet."

We had no difficulty in carrying him in and laying him on the divan in the living room. He was a thin little man and in the light I could see that he was quite old. His pale face was wrinkled and wizened and his

4

hair and bushy eyebrows were gray. His black overcoat, which was unbuttoned, fell open as we picked him up and disclosed that his spidery body was clad in very well cut evening clothes. I could feel no beat in the heart under the glistening shirt front fastened with black pearl studs.

Just then Mother burst into the room, hastily tying the cord of her plaid wool bathrobe and looking like a startled child with her short white hair tumbling around her flushed face.

"Jim, darling, what's happening?" she gasped.

"This man was ill in a taxicab outside and I brought him in. There's nothing to be alarmed about, Mother. You'd better go back to bed."

"Dearie me, he does look bad. Shall I fix a hot water bottle or something? He looks awful cold. That young Barton fellow who rooms with the Mertons is a doctor. Why don't you call him down here?"

That seemed a good suggestion and I went to the phone while Mother disappeared into the kitchen to heat the water. I knew that hot water bottles wouldn't help, but that seemed as good a way as any to keep her occupied. The young doctor upstairs said he'd be right down. Then I put in a call to the police station.

The cabby looked most nervous as I turned away from the phone. "Can I go now?" he asked.

"No," I replied shortly. "You'll wait until the police arrive."

Mother came in just then with a steaming hot water bottle. "Why, Jim, you haven't taken off his shoes or undone his collar or anything," she cried, and began pulling at one polished black slipper. Then she stopped suddenly. "Jim, I think he's dead!"

"Yes, Mother," I said quietly.

The bell rang and I admitted the excited and disheveled young doctor from upstairs who was closely followed by two blue-coated officers from district headquarters. The doctor moved immediately to the figure on the couch and lifted a limp head.

"Are you McBride who called the station house?" asked the first officer. "You say you found this man in a taxi and don't know who he is?"

"That's right."

"And who is this?" indicating young Barton.

"I am Dr. Barton. I live upstairs. Mr. McBride called me to come down to see if I could do anything for this man. I can't. He's been dead at least half an hour."

"So!" The officers began to appear more interested. "What did he die of, do you think?"

"It is impossible to tell without a complete examination, of course. It might have been heart failure, but there's something about the distortion of his face and body which makes me suspect that he might have been poisoned."

"Oh, dear, oh, dear! How awful!" cried Mother, hastily sliding a sofa cushion over the hot water bottle.

"Who is this?" asked the officer glaring toward the unhappy cab driver who was standing at the window staring out at his cab.

"He drove the cab that brought the man here," I put in as the driver seemed unable to speak.

"H'm-m," muttered the officer. "The medical examiner will be here soon. I put in a call for him before I left. You don't any of you know who the old guy is, huh? Did you look for identification on him?"

"No," I answered. "I didn't touch him again after I realized that he was dead. I thought I'd better wait until you came."

"Right. That the cab he came in standing outside?"

"Yes."

"Daly, you go out and see if there's anything in the cab, while I go through the old man's pockets," said the cop to his brother officer, and began fumbling in the dead man's clothes.

The pocket of the black overcoat yielded nothing but a clean white linen handkerchief with the initials J. C. In the pocket of his dinner jacket, however, were three folded slips of white paper. The cop spread them out on the table while I looked over his shoulder. They appeared to be notes written in a bold, masculine hand with thick, black pencil. They were all signed, "Signor Smeraldo." The first one read: "Come into the lobby after this act, I must see you"; the second: "I mean you no harm. Why do you avoid me? I must speak to you"; the third: "I will have a car waiting for you at the end of this act. If you come with me, all will be well. This is urgent."

"Signor Smeraldo, eh! Never heard it before, did you?" and he thrust the notes into his pocket and went on with the search.

There was some loose change and a gold pen-knife in the trouser pockets and a neatly folded crisp five-dollar bill in the pocket of the dress vest. That was all.

"None of that helps much," said the officer, "but he ought to be easy to spot as soon as the shops open. His soup and fish and his derby both came from Fifield's. Looks like he's a rich guy and lives right here in Chi. You don't suppose he's Signor Smeraldo, do you?"

"I shouldn't think so. The notes were evidently sent to him by this Smeraldo person. Besides his initials are J. C."

The cop then turned to the cabby who was cowering at the front windows gazing mournfully at his cab.

"You the fellow who drove the old gent out here?"

"Yeah," replied the cabby; "and the meter read $5.35 and I'd like to get my money and go along home. It's a long drive back and past time now for me to be in. The missus will worry."

"You'll stay right here until we get some more dope on this. What's your name?"

"Casimir Tiedeman. You don't think I done it, do you?"

"Not yet. Tell me just what happened from the time you picked up this fare until you got here."

"There ain't much to tell. I was parked in front of the Congress, about one o'clock I think it was. I wasn't tryin' to get fares 'specially because it was most time for me to turn my cab in for the night. This man just come along and got in."

"Did he come out of the hotel?"

"I dunno. I was dozin' a bit on my seat, I guess. I kinda got the idea that he came from the hotel, but maybe that was just because I was parked there by the entrance."

"You say he was already getting into the cab when you noticed him?"

"Yeah. He opened the door and kinda fell in. I guess he was sick then already. I thought maybe he was drunk or somethin'. I asked him what address and he just said 'home' first in a low voice so I could hardly hear it. 'Where's that?' says I, and then he says, '1887 W Street, Oak Park' in a louder voice, perfectly clear. I thought since his voice sounded all right, everything was okay and started off. I wasn't so keen about this trip, all the way out to Oak Park, so late on slippery streets and the snow freezin' to the windshield and no chance of a fare back to town either, but I couldn't turn him down very well."

"Did you speak to your passenger again on the way out, check the address or anything?"

"No, I don't hardly ever have to ask twice."

"Did you look around or notice anything peculiar about the way he acted?"

"No. Well, yes, I did look around once. I thought I heard the door of the cab slam and I was afraid maybe he'd jumped out without paying. I had a guy do that once. I had to stop sudden for a red light and the car was slidin' and then I heard this noise and looked around but the old guy was sittin' quiet in the corner of the cab. So I thought I musta been mistaken and drove on."

"What happened when you arrived at this address?"

"I asked if this was the right place and he didn't answer, so I got out and opened the door. He didn't move. I thought he'd gone to sleep, so I reached in and shook him some and his head wobbled funny and his hat fell over on his nose. I was scared then. I went in the building and rang the bell of the only apartment that still had a light in it. I thought they'd know where he belonged."

"Do you know anything about these slips of paper?"

"No, sir." Casimir Tiedeman scanned the crumpled notes that the officer drew from his pocket, but he kept his hands behind him and did not try to take the papers.

"This says something about the last act. Did you pick up any fares from a theater tonight?"

"No. I wasn't in the Loop theater time."

"Who were your fares before this bird?"

"A young couple been makin' whoopee at the Apex Club out South. I drove 'em to the Congress and was just standin' there waitin' for it to be time to check in when this gent came along."

"Does this check with what you know?" asked the officer, turning to me.

"Yes," I answered. "I went out to the cab after the man rang my bell."

7

"What was the appearance of the body when you first saw it?"

"The man was huddled into the far corner of the cab. His overcoat was unbuttoned and twisted under him and his hat was tilted forward on his nose."

"Do you remember whether his coat was unbuttoned when he got into the cab?" asked the officer, turning again to the taxi driver.

"I don't just remember, but it was snowin' and blowin' and he shoulda been buttoned up."

"H'm," muttered the cop, turning to young Barton. "He could have unbuttoned his own coat couldn't he?"

"It is possible, of course," answered Nesbit. "But if he were already ill when he got into the cab, it seems unlikely that he would have."

"Say, can't I go now? I live way out South and it's awful late," pleaded the unhappy taxi-driver.

"Write your name and address and the company you work for on this card," said the officer, "and then you can go. But you'll have to leave your cab to be examined in daylight."

"Jeez, officer," wailed the man, "it'll take me mosta the night to get home from here on the "L" and I'll get the devil for not turnin' my car in. It's goin' to do me a lotta harm anyway, gettin' mixed up in this kinda business. Even if I ain't suspected, it's likely to get into the news-papers and folks don't like to ride in cabs that other folks has died in. And how about my $5.35?"

The unfortunate man scrawled the desired information on the card; I looked over his shoulder and made note of the address myself. Then we all went out to the cab and made an examination of it as best we could with the inside light and a flashlight. It yielded nothing but a couple of wire hairpins and a candy wrapper. The ash-container held nothing but cigarette butts. The officers were sealing the cab with gummed paper for further investigation when the medical examiner drove up in the ambulance to take the unidentified body to the morgue. We followed him back into the apartment where Barton and Mother had remained with the body. The taxi-driver trudged way into the night.

The medical examiner made a cursory investigation, conferred with Dr. Barton, asked me a few questions, and then called his orderlies to carry the body away. My mysterious midnight visitor departed in his gruesome equipage for his gruesome destination. The officers left also, and Mother and I were alone again.

"Dear me, the poor man!" sighed Mother. "I hope they find out who he is and let his family know. His wife may be sitting up waiting for him now. But there's no reason why we should lose any more sleep about it. Come, get to bed, Jim darlin', or you'll be dead tired tomorrow morning."

"It's tomorrow morning now for me," I said. "I know that I'm a columnist and not a reporter, but when any kind of a newspaperman has a good story drive right up to his front door, that's no time for sleeping, Mother mine. It won't do me a bit of harm down at the office to get a scoop on this. Go fix me a cup of coffee and a sandwich like a good girl. I got in on the ground floor of this business and I'd like to stay there. I'm going over to the morgue as soon as I take a shower and have a bite to eat."

"You work on a newspaper and you lose all human sympathy. You don't think of anything but getting a story," grumbled Mother, but she trotted obediently off to the kitchen and soon the satisfying aroma of hot coffee filled the apartment. I called the office, found McNeil still at the night desk, told him what little I knew about the mysterious man in the taxi, then dashed for a shower.

Mother and I ate ham sandwiches and gulped hot black coffee at the kitchen table. It was a midnight snack for her and breakfast for me as she went back to bed and I started off as soon as the cab I called for arrived.

At the mortuary I found that I was still running in luck in this case. The first person I encountered was Inspector Ed Daggett. If Daggett had been called in on this case, it meant that it looked big.

"Hello, Jim," said Daggett curtly; "I've geen expecting you to show up. This stiff was left on your doorstep, I hear."

"Yeah. Have they found out who he is?"

"No, but he's no ordinary bum. That's plain from his clothes. Those studs of his are genuine black pearls. They're doing an autopsy now. Dr. Briggs thought it looked like a poisoning case and if we waited for identification and consent of the family the effects might wear off; some poisons have to be caught quick. I'm waiting for the report now."

"Have you seen him?"

"No, they'd already started the autopsy when I arrived and I decided I'd better keep out of the way. Seems as if I ought to know by sight any old gent around Chicago who can wear real black pearls in his shirtfront."

At this moment, Briggs, the medical examiner appeared.

"Well, inspector," he said slowly, "looks like you have a murder case on your hands. The man died of heart failure, auricular fibrillation brought on by a large dose of extract of strophanthus."

"What's that?" asked Daggett.

"It is a glucoside used as a cardiac stimulant, a form of digitalis, but dangerous in large doses, though not always fatal. The old man probably had a bad heart."

"H'm-m," muttered Daggett. "If the man had gone to bed instead of going out in a taxi and died during the night, this might have passed off as a natural death, case of heart failure, eh?"

"It is very likely," said the examiner. "That is what happens in a great many poisoning cases. The family doctor is called too late, signs the death certificate, and you and I never hear anything about it. But this time we know it's murder—or suicide."

"It doesn't seem likely that a man would take poison and then go riding around in a taxicab to an address where no one knew him, does it?" I queried.

9

"No, it doesn't. But we can't tell much about that until we find out who he is and where he thought he was going."

"No relatives called in to report that grandpa is missing?"

"No," snapped Daggett. "Well, can I go in and see the body now?"

"I think so," replied the examiner. "Come along, this way."

I followed them as unobtrusively as possible into the large, bare room strongly scented with disinfectants. On a wheeled table covered with a sheet lay my midnight visitor. His wizened little face appeared more placid now that the staring eyes were covered by the fine, wrinkled lids.

Daggett stared at him, groping for recognition. "I know I've seen that man somewhere or pictures of him, at least. Wait—I've got it! It's Jonathan Crane. He's a broker in La Salle Street and his wife gets into the society page pretty frequently, though he's a retiring old cuss."

"Sure, I remember her," said I; "a big blonde. The *Herald* ran a picture of her in the rotogravure last Sunday when she sang at a benefit bridge or something out on the North Shore. They live on Astor street, I think."

"Jonathan Crane," Daggett went on. "That fits the initials on the handkerchief and the get-up and everything. Well, thanks, Briggs; I've got to be getting on."

"Where are you going?" I asked.

"I'm going to Astor Street. I want to be on the premises when that household hears the news. It's often important to see how they take it."

"Don't you think that since Mr. Crane was deposited on my couch, he is sort of my responsibility and I ought to go along with you?"

"Your thoughtfulness is touching. Come on, if you like. But don't you go phoning anything to that paper of yours, until we make sure that it is Jonathan Crane."

CHAPTER 2

IT was a little before six o'clock on that foggy, bleak November morning that Inspector Daggett and I climbed out of our taxi at the curb of the tall narrow house of dark red brick on Astor Street. It looked chilly and unfriendly in the murky dawn. Was Jonathan Crane lying quietly asleep in the fastness of this dignified house, or was he lying stark and cold under the sheet of a mortuary cot? I felt a strange reluctance to mount those steps, hung back a bit and perhaps that is how I came to notice something that Daggett didn't.

"Wait a minute," I cried, as he started toward the house. "What time did it start to snow last night?"

"The rain changed to snow about midnight. Why? Oh, I see."

The snow on the white stone steps had already begun to melt away at the edges, but two sets of foot-prints showed up clearly as having been the last to be made—the prints of a flat-heeled shoe and a dainty slipper with a French heel, descending the steps.

"It would seem" said I, "that a man and a girl left the house about one o'clock and no one has come in since, as there are no ascending prints."

"Very good, Watson."

"And while I'm sleuthing, what about these?"

At the side of the house where a narrow passageway ran between the Crane house and its neighbor, I noticed more footprints, made about the same time as the others, judging from the amount of snow which had fallen before and after the print had been made. We walked over and looked at them more closely. There was a well shaped masculine tread going in and a splayed-out heel-less print overlaying it, coming toward the street.

"It would seem that a man walked in here and ran out a few minutes later in a considerable of a hurry. Prints made at the same time as the others."

"Excellent, Watson," said Daggett with some sarcasm, but he followed me down the alleyway with interest. We moved carefully along the edge of the walk so as not to disturb the footprints which ended abruptly under a little balcony which jutted out from the Crane house. Its floor was about level with a man's eyes. There was an iron grill work railing around it and by means of this I swung myself up. There was very little snow on the small floor of the balcony, but enough to show that a man had stood there the night before, had walked up the alley, swung himself up to the balcony probably as I had, stood a few minutes and then dashed out in a hurry.

French doors, closed and heavily curtained in dark red, gave upon the balcony. I tried one and to my great surprise it swung open. I had a glimpse of a long dark room lined with books, then pulled the door to again. No use creating a bad impression by sneaking in the windows when we had a perfect right to ring the doorbell and be admitted properly.

"The man climbed up on the balcony all right," I explained to Daggett as I climbed down again. "You can see toe prints in that little drift of snow by the doors. No way to tell whether he got in or not, but he could have, for the door isn't locked."

"You mean it isn't locked now," muttered Daggett. "That is funny. People in this neighborhood are usually very careful about locking up. It is a good thing we noticed those prints. They'll be melted in another hour."

We went back to the front steps, mounted them and rang the big bronze bell. We could hear it echoing through the quiet house but for some time there was no answering stir. After the third peal, the door was opened by a middle-aged man wearing garments obviously donned in haste and a most displeased expression.

"Is Mr. Jonathan Crane in?" asked Daggett.

"Yes, he's in," replied the man, "but he is not up. He never wakes before eight o'clock. You had better call later." He was about to close the door in our faces when Daggett stopped him.

"I am Inspector Daggett of Police Headquarters and this is Mr. McBride. We have reason to believe that Mr. Crane is not at home, that he did not return last night. A man who has been identified as Jonathan Crane was found dead in a taxicab in Oak Park last night. Will you please go up to his room and find out whether or not he is there."

"Come in, sir," said the man, his frigid annoyance turned to fear and alarm. "If you will just step into the reception room, I'll go upstairs at once and see if Mr. Crane is there."

He showed us into a small formal room at the left of the hall, decorated in a Frenchy style with gilt furniture and tapestry. Its dainty elegance seemed particularly inappropriate to our grisly errand and the bleak morning light.

"I prefer the room across the hall," I whispered. "Let's go in there. Unless I mistake the layout that is the room that opens on the balcony and I'd like to see if last night's visitor left anything behind him." We slipped quietly across the hall into the opposite room. The door was closed but not locked. The room was very dim. Daggett found the switch and the room filled with light from a big inverted bowl hung from the ceiling. It was a large handsome apartment but with a comfortable shabbiness as if nothing had been changed or renovated for a long time. My eyes wandered with interest to the books in the tall walnut cases, but Daggett's attention was immediately fixed on a small tray lying on the desk.

"Look at this, Jim," he said in an excited whisper.

It was a small silver tray on which stood two glasses, one tall and one squat, and a plate containing three sandwiches, the edges of the bread dried and curled back to reveal a filling of caviar.

"No, don't touch them," cautioned Daggett, as I started to pick up one of the glasses. "We may want fingerprints."

"Is it all right to smell them?" I asked with a sniff into each glass. "H'm, the tall boy here held a highball. Must have been good stuff, too, still to have a good odor of Scotch this morning, and the person who drank it finished off everything but the ice, at that. The little fellow, his drink smells like medicine to me, and looks green and sticky. There are advantages in arriving early before the house is cleaned up, aren't there, even if one doesn't get a warm reception."

Daggett had walked over to the French windows at the back of the room. The velvet drapes were pulled across them but they swung open easily, disclosing the little balcony with its iron railing and the blank wall of the next house. The fragmentary footprints were still discernible.

"The doors bolt from the inside, but the bolt isn't drawn. No handle outside but the doors open in and could be pushed easily enough from the balcony if they weren't locked. If that fellow came in last night, he must have had snow on his shoes. This deep napped carpet ought to

12

show something."

We both got down on our hands and knees and began examining the carpet in front of the glass doors. We failed to hear the returning footsteps of the butler on the stairs. He apparently had looked for us in the reception room where he had deposited us. Not finding us there and seeing the light under the library door, he flung it open and caught us in this undignified position.

"Did you lose something, gentlemen?" he queried icily.

"Oh, no," I said as pleasantly as possible. "We were just trying to find something."

"Mr. Crane's bed has not been slept in," he announced heavily as we scrambled to our feet.

"So!" said Daggett under his breath, then to the butler. "Can you tell me what Mr. Crane was wearing last night?"

"He was wearing dinner clothes, sir. He and Mrs. Crane attended the opera." (The opera; that's where he got those notes.)

"Can you describe his shirt studs?"

"They were black pearls—very fine ones, I believe."

"That about settles it," said Daggett, "though of course the body will have to be formally identified by some member of the family. The man in the taxi was Jonathan Crane."

"This is horrible! Unthinkable!" cried the butler in obvious distress. "Mr. Crane was well and in good spirits last night. I can hardly believe that such a thing is possible."

"Is Mrs. Crane in the house?"

"Yes, sir. She is still asleep in her room—that is, I hope she is," he added rather wildly, as if he could no longer be sure of anything.

"Mrs. Crane must be informed immediately."

"I think it would be best to inform Violet and have her break the news to Mrs. Crane. Violet is her personal maid. That would be more suitable, would it not? Dear, dear, the servants will take this hard too. We were all very fond of Mr. Crane."

"Very well, go and get Violet and come back here as soon as possible. There are several things I'd like to ask you. No, leave that tray here," Daggett commanded sharply as the butler, somewhat apologetically, went over to remove it.

Daggett and I continued our inspection of the room but the butler returned with such promptitude that we were unable to do any more sleuthing.

"Sit down," said Daggett. "I'd like to ask you a few questions before Mrs. Crane comes in. First of all, what is your name?"

"John Virtue."

"How long have you been with the Cranes?"

"It was twelve years ago that Mr. Crane employed me as his personal valet. That was before he was married. After he and Mrs. Crane were married and came back to this house, Mr. Crane took me on again as butler, though I still take care of his clothes. He doesn't have a regular valet any more."

"How long ago did Mr. Crane marry?"

"Six years ago last May. They were married in Italy and stayed abroad all summer. They took this house when they came back in the fall. It had belonged to Mr. Crane's family, but he hadn't lived in it when he was a bachelor. He preferred a smaller place."

"Were you with Mr. Crane when he married?"

"No. He didn't take me with him. I had decided to stay behind and go into business with some money I had saved up, but I wasn't very successful and was glad to return to him when he and Mrs. Crane came back to Chicago.

"Now, Virtue, will you tell me, as exactly as you can remember, everything that Mr. Crane did last evening."

"You talk as if— What was the cause of Mr. Crane's death, inspector?"

"He was poisoned," replied Daggett sharply. "If you were attached to your master, you will do everything you can to help us find out who was responsible for his death."

"Oh, yes, sir, indeed, sir!" stammered Virtue. He had gone very pale at Daggett's blunt announcement and looked genuinely bewildered. "But I don't understand it at all. It must have been some horrible accident. No one could have wished to kill Mr. Crane!"

"Apparently you are wrong there, but I asked you a question."

"Yes, yes, of course; you want to know what Mr. Crane did last evening. There was nothing out of the ordinary. Mrs. Crane had invited guests for dinner and the opera. She has a very fine voice herself and studied singing abroad at one time. She's been attending the opera quite frequently since the Chicago Civic Opera re-opened the first of the month. Well, last night was *Rigoletto* and Mrs. Crane is particularly fond of that opera because it reminds her of her first honeymoon in Italy."

"Her first one?"

"Yes, Mrs. Crane's first husband was an Italian nobleman. She was living in Italy as a widow when Mr. Crane met her. They spent their honeymoon in Italy, too, but I don't imagine they went to opera much, because Mr. Crane doesn't care for it. Last night was a special party, though, and she persuaded him to go."

"Who were the guests at dinner?"

"Mrs. Crawford Dawson, a widow who is a friend of Mrs. Crane, and her daughter were invited to dinner and to go to the opera with them, and Mr. Paige, Mr. Crane's nephew, was asked as a partner for Miss Dawson. After the opera, Mr. Paige came home with the Cranes, but the Dawsons had their own car meet them at the opera and went on. They live in Winnetka. Mrs. Crane went upstairs as soon as they got in and the two men went into the library. Mr. Crane brought out his collection of jewels—he has some very rare pieces you know—and Jerry, Mr. Paige, wanted to see them. He's seen them before, of course, but he always asks Mr. Crane to get them out for him when he comes here. He's always been crazy about looking at them since he was a

14

little chap. They had some sandwiches and something to drink in the library and then Mr. Jerry went home. Briscombe, Mr. Crane's chauffeur, waited and drove him to his apartment over on Surf Street."

"Are these the glasses they used?" asked Daggett, pointing to the tray on the desk."

"Yes, sir. Mr. Crane told me I could go after I had served them, so the tray didn't get carried out and you came so early, sir!"

"Don't apologize. It is more than all right with us. What did the gentlemen have to drink?"

"I brought in a whiskey and soda for Mr. Jerry, but Mr. Crane said he didn't want anything; he'd just drink his medicine."

"What was this medicine?"

"It is a tonic he has been taking for the last few weeks since he had the flu. He keeps it there in the left-hand drawer of the desk and takes a small glassful every evening before he goes to bed."

Daggett pulled open the indicated drawer and disclosed a squat pint bottle about half full of green liquid. He lifted it out in gingerly fashion with thumb and forefinger about its neck and placed it on the tray with the glasses.

"Who made the sandwiches?" he asked.

"I did," said Virtue.

"Did you open a fresh can of caviar?"

"Yes, sir."

"What did you do after you had served the gentlemen?"

"I went upstairs to bed, sir."

"You didn't lock up the house last night?"

"No, sir. Briscombe came in after I had gone up and he locked up the back door. Mr. Crane puts the night bolt on the front door when he remembers it. He's sometimes careless about locks, but the night latch is always on so that the door is locked outside and the extra bolt isn't necessary. Anyway we never have had any trouble."

"What about the French doors in the library?"

"I bolted them myself last evening."

"They were open when we tried them just now."

The butler looked most surprised. "Mr. Crane may have opened them again and forgotten to rebolt them. I had built a fire in here and it was rather warm. He may have opened them to get a little air. He's great for cool rooms and fresh air. Mr. Crane is—or was. Dear, dear, I can't believe that he is gone."

"Would he be likely to open the doors to get some air and forget to lock them for the night?"

"Oh, yes, he's done that before. It's a bad neighborhood for thieves too, but we've never had any."

"You did not know that Mr. Crane went out again last night?"

"No, I didn't know he had gone out. But I remember now I did hear something; I'd almost forgotten about it. I went upstairs—I sleep on the fourth floor at the front—and noticed the car waiting at the curb for Mr. Jerry, as I went to pull down the shade. Pretty soon I heard

15

the motor start and thought Mr. Crane would be locking up and hoped he wouldn't want anything. Then, just as I was getting into bed, I heard the doorbell ring. There's an extension up to the servant's rooms on the fourth floor, so I heard it very plain even though it seemed like a short timid ring and wasn't repeated. I got up and went to the window and saw a taxi in front of the house. The bell didn't ring again so I knew Mr. Crane must have answered it. I was puzzled, because I couldn't imagine who it could be; Mr. Crane never has late visitors.

"I stood at the window for a few minutes and then I saw another car drive up and park at the curb two houses down from us. It was snowing and I could just see the headlights shining on the thick flakes; I couldn't tell what kind of a car it was or anything. Then a man came walking up the street. I'm not sure whether he got out of the car or not. I had an idea that he did, but maybe that was just because it was the only car and he was the only man on the street and I put them together. He walked past the other two houses, stopped a minute out in front here, then suddenly ducked into the little passageway between this house and the Allens' next door. I watched a few minutes longer, but the man didn't come back and no one left the house. My feet were cold so I went back to bed. I didn't hear anyone go out."

"Is it unusual for anyone to use that passageway?"

"Not especially. It goes right on through to a gate that opens on the alley at the back. People use it once in a while when they want a short cut to the alley and the chauffeur uses it occasionally."

"Would anyone but yourself have been likely to have seen this?"

"None of the other servants. My room is the only one at the front of the house and the others were all asleep except Briscombe who came in later."

"Would Mrs. Crane have heard the bell?"

"Not if she'd gone to sleep. It wasn't a very loud ring and you can't hear the bell very well from the bedrooms on the third floor anyway."

"Were the two cars still there when you went back to bed?"

"Yes."

"As we came in," said Daggett slowly, "we noticed in the snow footprints of a man and a woman, evidently the last persons to leave the house last night. Mr. Crane's visitor must have been a woman and he must have accompanied her on a ride from which he was never to return alive. Have you any idea who that woman could have been?"

"No, sir, not the slightest. Mr. Crane didn't have any woman friends that I know of, and his only relative in this part of the country is his nephew, Jerry Paige. I couldn't imagine who could be coming and ringing the doorbell at that time of night. It must have been around one o'clock."

"And both cars were still parked in the block when you went away from the window?'

"Yes, sir. The taxi at the door and the other down the block."

"Are you sure that the second car wasn't Mr. Crane's car returning?"

"Quite sure, it looked like a smaller car and the lights were different.

16

Besides Briscombe drove in the alley and put the car away a few minutes later."

"Did you hear him come in?"

"Yes; he entered by the back way as usual."

"Do you know whether or not Mr. Crane knows anyone by the name of Smeraldo?"

"I've never heard the name. I'm quite sure no one by that name ever came to the house. Mr. Crane might have known him in some outside connection, of course."

"That's all for the present, Virtue. I'm going to take the things on this tray along with me. Will you get me a box and some paper to wrap them in?"

Virtue gave Daggett a swift startled look, but answered, "Yes, sir," and left the room.

On a sudden impulse I jumped up and followed at his heels. "Just going to look around," I said over my shoulder to Daggett as I went out.

Virtue didn't seem overpleased to have my company, but he said nothing. I followed him down the stairs to the ground floor, through a well stocked butler's pantry into the kitchen. The other servants had not come downstairs yet and the big room was clean and chilly and bare. The only mar to its neatly scrubbed appearance was a track of muddy footprints from the back door across the linoleum floor to the back stairs.

"Who tracked in all this mud?" I asked.

"Briscombe, I imagine. He came in last night after Mrs. Bruns had cleaned up for the night," Virtue answered coldly. He evidently did not approve of this invasion of the kitchen.

"If I had to scrub these floors, I'd teach him to wipe off his feet when he came in," I went on still gazing at the muddy prints. "Is Briscombe usually so untidy?"

"I don't know," muttered Virtue, fishing in a drawer for paper and string. "Is there anything more you wish to see or shall we return to Mr. Daggett?"

I shrugged amiably and we climbed to the library. Daggett was just putting up the telephone on the desk. "I've sent Oliver over to the Congress to get any dope he can on a woman who was escorted there after one o'clock by Jonathan Crane or about a Signor Smeraldo. I'm staying here to interview the rest of the house."

"All right, I'll stay with you," said I.

CHAPTER 3

DAGGETT had just finished his careful wrapping of the medicine bottle, the glasses and the sandwiches when Virtue announced Mrs. Crane. One of the qualities which made that lady such a popular clubwoman in the city was her unfailing ability to make an effective entrance, and this art did not desert her even under the tragic circumstances of that November morning. We both caught our breaths as she swept in, a statuesque, glittering woman clad in a trailing robe of black velvet stenciled in gold and bound with a curious girdle of woven gold.

She acknowledged Daggett's introductions with properly repressed graciousness and sank into the leather armchair which Daggett drew forward for her. In spite of her poise and glitter, I fancied I detected a look óf strain and anxiety on her face, more akin to terror than to grief.

"Violet has told me of the dreadful news you bring," she said in a low richly toned voice, "and I am still almost unable to believe it. I left my husband well and happy only a few hours ago, and to be awakened with this horrible and incredible story—You must pardon me, gentlemen, if I am somewhat shaken."

"We are very sorry indeed, madam, to have had to awaken you with such bad news and to intrude ourselves upon your grief in this way," said Daggett, and hurriedly reviewed the discovery of Jonathan Crane. "Does the Oak Park address mean anything to you?"

"Nothing whatever. I have no friends in Oak Park and have no knowledge that my husband had any, surely none that he would call on at two o'clock in the morning. Have you determined the cause of death?"

"Your husband died of heart failure brought on by an overdose of extract of strophanthus."

"Are you sure?" cried the widow. Her graceful figure which had been drooping in the big armchair was suddenly erect and tense, and her sapphire-blue eyes were wide with horror or fright, I wished that I could know which.

"It is quite definitely established," replied Daggett. "Our present duty is to find out who administered the poison."

"Of course," breathed the widow. "But it all seems quite incrediblè."

"You know of no one who would wish your husband's death?"

"No, he had no enemies, unless they were business rivals of whom I knew nothing. He was a quiet, solitary, but very kindly man."

"Did you know that your husband intended going out again last evening?"

"No, I had no idea of it. Did he leave with Jerry?"

"No, he did not leave with Mr. Paige," Daggett replied. "We learned

18

from the butler that Mr. Crane had a caller after Mr. Paige left. Virtue had gone to bed but he heard the doorbell ring and saw a taxi parked at the curb. You did not hear the bell?"

"No, I heard nothing after I went upstairs. I was tired and went to sleep immediately. Virtue did not come down or see who the visitor was?"

"No, he said the bell rang only once, rather feebly. He assumed that Mr. Crane had answered and went back to bed. However, when we arrived this morning there were two clear sets of footprints descending your front steps, those of a man and a woman. It is to be supposed that your husband left the house last night about one o'clock in the company of a woman wearing small, high-heeled slippers and that they went to the Congress Hotel, as that is where the taxi-driver picked up Mr. Crane about half an hour later. Have you any idea who that woman could have been?"

The blue gaze which the widow turned upon us both was so frankly incredulous that it was apparent that whatever may have been the faults of the late Mr. Crane he was not, at least to his wife's knowledge, a philanderer.

"I know of no friend of myself or my husband who is staying at the Congress Hotel at present, and I cannot imagine who the woman could have been. My husband did not care for the company of women as a rule and had no women friends who would call upon him informally at that hour of the night."

"Do you know anyone by the name of Smeraldo?"

"No!" answered the widow with a puzzled little frown. "I've never heard the name."

"These notes were found in your husband's pocket." Daggett handed her the folded scraps of paper.

I noticed a faint start of surprise as the woman's eyes fell upon the heavy black-penciled words of the note. She read it in tense silence and handed it back to Daggett, her blue eyes blank and opaque.

" I know of no such person."

"Did your husband receive a note during the performance?"

"No. He and Jerry went out for a smoke after the second act. He might have received a note then, but except for that interval I am sure that he could not have received a note without my noticing it."

"Did anyone stop you on the way out or speak to Mr. Crane?"

"We nodded to some friends but didn't stop. We were in a hurry to get out in order to find the car before the crowd was too dense."

"Nothing unusual happened at the opera?"

"Nothing at all."

"Your husband and your nephew Jerry Paige are on good terms, I suppose?"

"Oh, yes. Jonathan was very fond of the boy. Jerry has been trying to borrow money of him lately in order to buy into a practice in Evanston. Mr. Crane refused him, partly because his own affairs are a bit involved at present and partly because he felt that things have always

19

come too easy to Jerry and it would be good for him to fight his own way up instead of just buying something ready made. He is a house physician now at one of the hospitals. Jerry was disappointed at the refusal, but showed no hard feeling."

"Your husband, I believe, had a fine collection of jewels?"

"Yes," said the widow curtly.

"Where does he keep the collection?"

"In the safe in this room. He was showing it to Jerry last night."

"I think it would be wise to see if the collection is still intact this morning. You are familiar with all the pieces, of course?"

"Oh, yes, I am familiar with them, but I cannot open the safe for you. Mr. Crane was the only one in the house who had the combination. The safe is in the wall behind that portrait of Uncle Aaron Crane."

"I have a pretty good feel for combinations if the safe isn't too tricky," I said. "Mind if I see if I can get this one?"

I moved over to the dark old portrait of an irascible-looking gentleman in a high wing collar, lifted the heavy gold frame from the wall and uncovered the metal circle of the safe. "Go ahead and don't mind me," I said. "I'll have to tinker a bit. I'm not guaranteeing I can do it."

"I wasn't aware of this accomplishment," muttered Daggett. "Would you like a bit of sandpaper, Valentine?"

"No, thanks," I replied a bit abstractedly, as I already was working at the dials.

Mrs. Crane looked highly displeased but said nothing.

"I have seen only one of your servants, Virtue, the butler. What about the others?"

"There is Virtue; Violet, my maid; Mrs. Bruns, the cook; and Briscombe, the chauffeur; that is all."

"They are all perfectly trustworthy?"

"I think so, yes. Virtue and Mrs. Bruns have been with us for five years, ever since we have lived here. Violet has been in my service for nearly a year and has been very satisfactory. Briscombe has been with me only a few months, but he came to me very highly recommended from a friend in the East for whom he had worked for several years. I have been completely satisfied with his services."

"I shall, of course, interview the other servants."

"Do anything you think best in the house," said Mrs. Crane languidly.

I interrupted this conversation with a sudden shout as the lock clicked and the metal circle in the wall swung out. There was nothing in the cavity but a brassbound casket of dark wood. I drew it out and laid it on the desk.

"Mr. Crane carries the only key," said Mrs. Crane with a disdainful sidelong glance at the casket.

"Perhaps it is in this lot," said Daggett, drawing from his pocket the leather key container he had found in the dead man's pocket. "We found these keys among Mr. Crane's effects last night," he explained to the widow, as he fitted a little brass key to the lock of the jewel box.

20

It turned easily, and he flung back the cover, disclosing a collection of black velvet cases. "You can tell us, I presume, whether all the jewels are here."

"Mr. Crane always kept a list in the drawer of his desk. You can check from that," said Mrs. Crane coldly. She rose and moved over to the desk, pulled out the left hand drawer. "Oh, the medicine bottle is gone. He always keeps it in this drawer."

"Yes," said Daggett. "I have it, madam."

"I see," she gave Daggett a long appraising glance, then began poking among the papers at the back of the drawer and produced a typewritten list. "Every piece is listed here with full description."

We began opening the cases and checking the items with the descriptions on the list. There was no time to stop and admire the glittering stones and beautiful workmanship so hastily revealed as we opened one case after another.

"They are all here," said Daggett, putting the last case back into place. "It wasn't jewels the murderer was after."

"I cannot accept the idea of murder," said Mrs. Crane. "My husband had a weak heart and had been warned against any excitement or strain. Are you sure that he could not have died from natural causes?"

"Strophanthus is hardly a natural food, madam, though perhaps it would not have been fatal if he had not had a weak heart. However, if he had gone straight to bed instead of venturing out in a taxicab, he might have died quietly at home and the cause of his death would never have been discovered."

"Yes, quite true," Mrs. Crane spoke rather dreamily, her mind was off somewhere examining this idea.

"He might, however, have taken his own life by drinking the poison intentionally. Do you know of any worries or difficulties that might have led him to take such an action?"

"I can hardly believe that—still it might be. . . . Really I—" The woman's voice trailed off into silence. Then she straightened to her former regal dignity and said in a cold clear voice, "You must excuse me now, please, gentlemen. I will do anything in my power to aid you in solving this horrible mystery which surrounds my husband's death, but at present I am too confused and sad to answer your questions coherently."

She turned and walked rapidly from the room before we could reply.

"Well," said Daggett, staring at the door rather disconcertedly, "what do you make of that?"

"She needs more time to think up her answers," I offered.

"You think she knows more than she is letting on?"

"Well, naturally. She was genuinely surprised on a few points; you could tell that. But she was pretty cagey and she won't talk until she is sure of her ground. She may not have a guilty conscience, but she has something on her mind, all right."

Daggett thought a moment, then said, "Stow that jewel box away, and we'll interview the rest of the crowd."

21

Virtue's prompt appearance at Daggett's ring suggested that he had not been far from the keyhole during our talk with Mrs. Crane. Daggett asked him to tell Mrs. Crane's maid to come to the library at once.

"Yes, sir, and there are two men waiting for you in the hall."

"That will be Pierce and his assistant. I'll go give him instructions and you wait here and catch Miss Violet."

Violet arrived shortly, a trim little figure of a girl in a gray dress and dainty white apron. She had smooth dark hair parted in the center and widely spaced hazel eyes, round with curiosity and excitement. "Oh," she said prettily, "are you a policeman?"

"No, just the policeman's helper," said I.

"Can I be of any help to a policeman's helper?"

We would have got along nicely with this inane dialogue if Daggett had not returned just then. She curtsied respectfully when she saw him but did not seem at all timid or frightened.

"You are Mrs. Crane's personal maid, I believe. I am Inspector Daggett and this is Mr. McBride. I'd like to ask you a few questions."

"Yes, sir."

"What is you name?"

"Violet Handsley."

"Your voice sounds English."

"Yes, sir. I came from Plymouth. Three years ago I came over as lady's maid to Mrs. Mowbry Newcombe. She engaged me in London and brought me back with her."

"How long have you been with Mrs. Crane?"

"A year next month it will be. Mrs. Newcombe was going out West and didn't want to take me with her. She let me go with a good reference and Mrs. Crane engaged me the next week."

"Are you satisfied with your place here?"

"Oh, yes, Mrs. Crane is a good mistress. She's never unkind, but then, she's never exactly kind either. Mrs. Newcombe used to talk to me a lot—tell me all about the party she'd been to when I was combing her hair for the night and ask my advice about things. But Mrs. Crane never says anything to me at all. It gets kind of lonesome upstairs and Cook isn't much company. I get good wages and all Mrs. Crane's old dresses, though I have to take them in so much it spoils the style of them. Mrs. Newcombe was just my size. I've thought sometimes of leaving the place just on account of the lonesomeness."

"I believe it was you who broke the news of her husband's death to Mrs. Crane."

"Yes, sir, and a harder thing I never had to do—waking a lady out of a sound sleep to tell her such a terrible thing as that."

"How did Mrs. Crane take the news?"

"Really, sir, you're asking some rather personal questions that I don't know as I ought to answer. Was there something wrong about Mr. Crane's dying that you should come and ask all the servants about how his family took it? I know it isn't regular to die in a taxicab, but was he—was there—"

"There were certain unusual circumstances about his death which we must clear up, and to do so we must get some information about Mr. Crane and his household."

"I wouldn't want to hold anything back if it was important. Well, as I said, she was sleeping. so I tiptoed in and called her name kind of softly a few times until she woke up. Then I told her just what Virtue had told me. She didn't cry or carry on any, but then, she wouldn't. She just looked sort of bewildered and scared. She sat there for a few minutes looking awful pale and then said, 'Oak Park. Why Oak Park?' I could have thought of some answers to that one, but I just said I didn't know.

"Then she asked what he had died of. I said they thought it was heart failure; that's what Virtue told me, and I said there were two men downstairs waiting to see her. She wanted to know who they were and I said it was a policeman and a reporter. Is that right? That's what Virtue told me. She didn't say anything more at all, just sat up in bed looking kind of rigid and puzzled while I laid out her things. She's not one to show her feelings much, but she probably feels just as bad as some who'd cry and tear their hair."

"Were she and Mr. Crane on good terms?"

"Oh, yes, as good as most rich people I've worked for. They never had much to say to each other, when I was around anyway, and they don't care for the same kind of things. She likes to go about and he doesn't care for society."

"Does she go alone then?"

"Sure, she's out a lot—luncheons and club stuff during the day and dinners and receptions in the evenings too."

"Does she go to such things alone or with other men?"

"Oh, both. She goes with other men sometimes, but I don't think there's any trouble about that. She makes no secret of it and the master doesn't seem to mind. She doesn't seem to have any trouble getting someone to take her out evenings when Mr. Crane won't go, but she never seems to concentrate on any one man or start any scandals, so far as I know, and it's hard to keep that sort of thing from your personal maid, you know."

"She and Mr. Crane never quarrel then?"

"I wouldn't say never, but not much. There's only one thing that they squabble over and they can start a fight about that any time it is mentioned."

"What's that?"

"Well, perhaps you've heard that Mr. Crane has a very grand collection of old jewelry, antique pieces with a history to them, you know. He's showed them to me a couple of times and they are gorgeous. He keeps them in velvet cases in his safe and won't let Mrs. Crane wear them. It makes her just furious because she doesn't see any reason why a man should put so much money into jewelry just to stow away in a safe. The stuff was made to be worn, she says, and the person to wear it is the wife of the owner. He won't argue with her or give her

23

any reasons; he just says nothing and doesn't open the safe for her. She simply fumes and I don't know as I blame her."

"Now, Miss Handsley," said Daggett, breaking into Violet's voluble explanations, "what did you do during the evening?"

"Well, really, does that make much difference?" said Violet, looking rather coy.

"Perhaps not," said Daggett, and then waited for the explanation which he was positive would be forthcoming.

"I suppose if you think it is important enough to ask at a time like this I'd better answer it," said Violet. "Well, I sewed some beads on one of Mrs. Crane's evening gowns until I heard Briscombe honking outside. Briscombe is the Crane's chauffeur. You see he can't park downtown very well so he told me he'd come back and we'd go to a movie to pass the time until the opera was over. We went over to the cinema on Chicago Avenue and saw some German picture. I didn't think so much of it but he wanted to see it for some reason or other."

"Do you and Briscombe go out together frequently?"

"Oh, quite a bit. It breaks the monotony to be interested in somebody around the house. I guess Briscombe feels the same. He's really quite a swell guy for a chauffeur. The one we had before him was old and had a wife already in a boarding house over on La Salle Street, and he was a pill anyway."

"Thank you very much, Miss Handsley. You will be in the house, I presume, in case we should want you again."

"Yes, sir," said Violet, rather taken aback that the interview should terminate just as it was beginning to get interesting.

Mrs. Bruns, when she appeared, proved to be a middle-aged woman, stout and plain, evidently sincerely grieved by the death of her master as well as considerably frightened by the presence of the police. However, she managed to tell her story clearly enough. She had been with the Cranes ever since they had returned from abroad five years ago. She had been at home most of the time in the kitchen, all of the preceding day, as Mrs. Crane had had lunch at home and there was a dinner party of six to prepare for in the evening. She hadn't finished in the kitchen until nine then had gone to bed with a copy of the *Ladies' Home Journal*. She turned out her lights at about ten o'clock and had heard nothing further. She admitted to being a bit deaf so that she seldom heard any of the bells in the house.

The chauffeur was called next. He was a tall, well built fellow. I was at a loss to place his age. His dark hair was gray at the temples, but his handsome brown eyes were youthful, as was his sleek, uniformed figure. He showed no signs of either excitement or distress, but told calmly how he had driven the Cranes and their guests to the opera, had come back to take Miss Handsley to a movie while he waited for the opera to close, had called again at the opera and driven Mr. and Mrs. Crane and Mr. Paige back to Astor Street.

"You waited outside for Mr. Paige?"

"Yes, sir."

24

"How long was Mr. Paige with his uncle?"

"About three-quarters of an hour."

"Where did you take Mr. Paige after he left here."

"Home to his apartment over on Surf Street."

"Did you return immediately after you had taken Mr. Paige home?"

"I stopped over on Clark Street to buy some cigarettes, that's all."

"Did you notice any other cars in the block or see anyone go into the house or up the passageway?"

"No, sir."

"Did Mr. Crane tell you to put the car up when you returned?"

"He didn't say anything about it, so I took it for granted that he was through with it for the night. He didn't say anything to me about going out again."

"Do you know whether Mr. Crane knows anyone by the name of Smeraldo?"

"I never heard it, sir, not as a name."

"Where did you drive the family during the day?"

"I drove Mr. Crane down to his office on La Salle Street at nine o'clock. I do that every morning; the rest of the day the car is usually at Mrs. Crane's disposal. The car wasn't called out again during the morning yesterday. At two-thirty I took Mrs. Crane for a drive; she stopped at a tea in Winnetka and returned home a little after five. In the evening I took them to the opera as I have told you."

"You didn't call for Mr. Crane?"

"No, I seldom do. He's uncertain about the hour he comes home and Mrs. Crane almost always uses the car in the afternoon."

"You have just the one car?" I put the question this time.

"Yes, an Isotta Fraschini town car."

"That can hardly occupy all your time. What did you do all morning, for instance?"

Briscombe looked rather annoyed at having a fellow like me who apparently was not in authority presuming to ask him personal questions, but he replied with dignity. "I sometimes help Virtue with some of the indoor work. This morning we polished the silver and brass."

"Did you polish that fender?" I asked, pointing to the gleaming brass before the marble fireplace.

"Yes," replied Briscombe shortly.

"Nice job," I said pleasantly.

"If that is all," said Briscombe, "I'd like you to excuse me. I have to drive Virtue out to the morgue to identify the body."

"That is all for the present. By the way, if you are going downtown, you might drop McBride and me off at the Congress Hotel."

"Very well, sir."

25

CHAPTER 4

DAGGETT had Briscombe drive first to an address on Dearborn Street where he left the bottle of green tonic, the glasses and the sandwiches to be analyzed by a chemist and examined for fingerprints, then we drove on to the Congress Hotel. A tall young man was standing at the desk engaged in earnest conversation with the room clerk. He looked around as Daggett and I entered and as his eye encountered Daggett's grimly enquiring look, he flushed unhappily.

"Well, Oliver?" said Daggett.

"I haven't been able to locate anything, Inspector," said the man. "There is no one registered here under the name of Smeraldo; I haven't found anyone who's ever even heard the name before. Some of the staff know Crane by sight but say they have never seen him in the hotel and no one of his description was seen here with a woman last night."

"Have you any leads on the woman?"

"Well, no, not so far. There isn't much to go on. There are so many people coming and going all the time in the lobby that I couldn't get anything very definite. But I have a list here of the women staying in the hotel who came in last night after midnight, as near as the night clerk could remember."

"Let's see that list," said Daggett impatiently.

I had modestly withdrawn from this discussion and was peering idly at the register, turning the page unobtrusively when the clerk's attention was otherwise engaged. An entry of the night before caught my attention. "Who is this?" I said putting a finger on one of the entries.

Daggett looked up from his list and glanced over at the register. "Mme. Emerande, Versailles," he read, from the signature written across the page in a flowing, graceful hand.

"I think that is a 'u' not an 'n'," I said, "making it Emeraude."

"Well, what of it? Do you know her? Does she mean Versailles, France, or Versailles, Indiana?"

"I don't know anything about her or her home town, but Signor Smeraldo means Mr. Emerald in Italian and Madame Emeraude means Mrs. Emerald in French. I thought it might be an international marriage or something."

"That's worth looking into," commented Daggett. She's probably the one meant by this item 'new French woman' on this list." And to the clerk, "Who is this Madame Emeraude?"

"I don't remember her," said the clerk. "She registered just yesterday afternoon. Do you want to ring her room?"

"Gosh, yes!"

26

The cashier who had been listening in on the conversation from his side of the desk, stepped over as he heard this and said, "There is no use ringing her. She checked out about half an hour ago. She paid her bill to me. I remember her perfectly."

"So, she's gone," said Daggett, glaring at Oliver.

"That must have been while I was upstairs talking to the night clerk," muttered Oliver.

"What can you tell me about her?" said Daggett to the cashier.

"She was young, about twenty-five, I should say, blond, and very simply dressed. She had on a black suit with some black fur on it, and a small black felt hat. She was very pretty but looked a bit shabby; that is, the suit wasn't the latest style and the fur was worn. I don't know that I would have noticed those things except that she was so unusually good-looking and most of the women who come here are well dressed. She had a small bag and insisted on carrying it herself, went out the side entrance with it in her hand."

"You don't know what she did last night, I suppose."

"No, I'm not on duty after six o'clock. The night clerk could probably tell you more about her."

"Go up and bring him down, Oliver," said Daggett shortly.

Daggett next called the doorman over and asked him if he remembered a young lady in a black suit who had left by the side entrance about half an hour before.

"Oh, yes, I remember her," replied that dignified, gold-braided individual. "She was carrying her own bag and said she didn't want a taxi. She was walking west still carrying the bag the last I saw of her."

"Did you notice anything else about her?"

"Nothing special. She was pretty, but frumpy-looking, if you get what I mean. Seemed a bit nervous, though that may have been because all the bellboys were trying to carry her bag and the whole row of taxis parked in front were offering her a ride."

"She was either stony-broke or a woman of great character," I observed. "It is no easy matter to carry your own bag out of a Loop hotel."

"It is just eight o'clock now," said Daggett. "She must have checked out before seven-thirty. Pretty early for a lady who'd been out the night before. She must have had something on her mind."

Oliver returned with a very annoyed-looking night clerk.

"What's the idea of all the hullabaloo about this woman?"

"I am Inspector Daggett from Headquarters and I want to get some information about a Madame Emeraude who was in the hotel last night and who left early this morning—a young blond woman. Do you recall seeing her in the lobby last evening?"

"Yes, I remember her because there was a man asking about her last night. She had dinner in the dining room here and when she came out a young chap who had been standing around in the lobby asked me who she was. I didn't know and anyway we don't supply information like that, so I didn't tell him anything. Then he said that she looked like an old friend of his that he hadn't seen for a long time and asked if he could look at the register and see if her name was there, because he didn't want to approach the lady if he was wrong. He took a look at the last page and said, 'Oh, yes, there it is, Madame Emeraude.' By that time she had gone. She got a taxi and went right out after dinner without going upstairs again."

"What time was that?"

"About eight-thirty. She went in to dinner late."

"What was she wearing?"

"A black dress with a black velvet cape over it. There was nothing very swell about her clothes, but you'd notice her anywhere. She wore no hat and she had lots of very fair hair."

"Did you see her come in again?"

"Yes, she came in about one-thirty. If she had an escort, she said good-by to him at the door, because she came into the lobby alone, got her key and went right upstairs."

"And this man who enquired about her—what did he look like?"

"He was a dark, good-looking chap, under thirty I should say. He had some sort of a foreign accent, might have been Spanish or Italian. I don't know who he was. I'd never seen him around the hotel before."

"Did you see him again that evening?"

"No."

"Did Madame Emeraude have a foreign accent?"

"She didn't sound foreign, though she didn't talk like a middle-Westerner exactly."

"I'd like to get in touch with the doorman who was on duty last night after midnight. Which entrance did she use?"

"The Michigan Avenue entrance. That would be Hodges. He's gone home, but I can get him for you on the phone."

While Daggett was engaged in telephoning the doorman, I went prowling on my own. I peered into the big glittering dining room across the lobby which was dim and deserted as was also the Joseph Urban Room down the corridor, but the grill room which looked out upon the wind-swept avenue was already bright and busy and a number of early risers were eating bacon and eggs behind their morning papers. I summoned the steward who came hurrying over with a menu to show me to a table.

"I don't want any breakfast. I'm from police headquarters," I said sternly. Both these statements were lies as I could have polished off Club Breakfast No. 5 on that menu with the greatest ease and I had no police badge. However, I got away with it for he immediately took on a serious and concerned expression and asked what he could do for me.

"I am trying to trace a woman who registered at the hotel yesterday under the name of Madame Emeraude. She dined here last evening, in the Joseph Urban Room I believe. I'd like to put a few questions to the waiter who served her."

"I was in the Joseph Urban Room at dinner last night. Can you

28

describe the woman? I might remember her."

"She was young and blond and wore a black velvet dinner gown. She dined alone, I think."

"Yes, I recall such a woman. She sat alone at a corner table, one of Pierre's. He doesn't come on until noon but he lives here. I'll have him called in."

I waited there, hungrily watching a portly old gentleman eat a large stack of fragrant cakes and syrup but I didn't dare order anything for fear Daggett would see me and walk out on me. I didn't want to be shaken just yet.

The steward returned presently with a gesticulating little Frenchman whom he introduced as Pierre Binet. "He says that he remembers your blond woman in black," the steward added.

"*Mais, oui!* A very beautiful blond young lady—I remember her well and hope she is not in any trouble. You say the police look for her?"

"Yes, but so far we've been looking in the wrong directions and she's disappeared. What can you tell me about her? Did you observe that she was a compatriot of yours, by the way?"

"What you mean?"

"Well, she signed the register as Madame Emeraude from Versailles. That sounds French to me."

"Ah, yes, she did talk to me in French—good Parisian French too, not the kind the most people talk to French waiters. But I did not know she was a *française;* she did not speak English like a French lady."

"H'm-m. Well, what else can you remember about her?"

"She was a very charming lady, most distinguish', you call it. She comes in about seven-thirty, all alone, and the headwater, he shows her to my table in the corner where she can see everything and yet is not too much noticed, you know, for a lady alone in the evening. I suggest to her all the finest things on the menu and she orders just what I tell her. It was a good dinner, *superbe*, and she seemed to like it very much and gave me a very nice tip at the end."

"Did she appear to be at all nervous or upset during dinner?"

"Oh, no; she appear very happy and pleased with everything. *Les yeux*, they sparkle and shine."

"*Quelle couleur, les yeux?*" I enquired.

"*Je ne sais pas exactement, mais*—. They must be blue to match her hair, thick fair hair in a simple coiffeur with a knot at the neck. No, but wait, I remember. Her eyes, they were green. Perhaps they seemed so because she wore a green *bijou*, what you call it—a necklace with a shining green stone."

"You've never seen her here before?"

"No, never any place. She is the sort of lady one does not forget."

"Did she know anyone in the dining room? Did you see her speak to any friend?"

"No, she seemed all alone and a little strange and timid, but a very lovely lady. I can't believe that she has done anything bad to make the police want her."

29

"Oh, no, we just want to ask her a question or two," I said reassuringly. "Good-by, Pierre, and thanks."

I went up and rejoined Daggett and Oliver in the lobby. Daggett glared at me and wanted to know where I had been. I told him briefly of my interview with Pierre, which had not contributed much to our search except to indicate that the lady was in good spirits and fine appetite at dinner time, which seemed to annoy Daggett.

"We're on the right track, all right," said Daggett. "Hodges, the man at the door last night, remembered seeing the woman go out alone in a taxi; he didn't hear the address. The young Italian that the night clerk mentioned tried to find out from him where she was going. He went off in a taxi too after he'd tried to pump the doorman about her. Hodges saw her come in; said she was walking with a slight old man about as tall as she was, wearing a black derby and overcoat. Description tallies perfectly with Crane. He said the man left her at the door and took a taxi that was standing out in front. That fits all right with Casimir Tiedeman's story. I wonder what they did with the car they left the Crane house in. She's the woman we're after though. Rotten break to have her get away. Oliver could have caught her if he'd had any sense. Hodges said he saw that foreign fellow hanging around again outside just before she got back. Wonder who he can be and where he fits into the picture."

"Maybe that's our friend, Mr. Emerald, alias Smeraldo," I suggested.

"Not a bad hunch," muttered Daggett.

A search of the room which had been occupied by Madame Emeraude and some further consultation with doormen and elevator boys revealed nothing more of importance concerning the mysterious woman in black.

"There's nothing more to do here at present," said Daggett. "I'll leave Oliver on the job, but I'm going over to see the nephew, young Paige."

"May I come along?" I asked. "I used to know Jerry pretty well on one of the occasions when I went to college, but I haven't seen anything of him for a long time."

"Come on, then, if you like. It might be a good idea to have you along to give the call a friendly look and not put the young chap too much on his guard. I called him and told him to wait at his apartment until I arrived. Virtue had already called to tell him about his uncle's death. Grab a taxi, will you?"

CHAPTER 5

"SO you went to college with this young Paige fellow," said Daggett as we were speeding northward once more. "I didn't know you'd ever been to college."

"Sure, how else did you suppose I knew how to say emerald in two different languages? It's a wonderful thing, a college education."

"What sort of a fellow is Paige?"

"Damn nice boy, awfully good-looking chap. The girls were always after him and a lot of them caught up with him, as I remember. I haven't seen him for years."

We fell silent until the taxi slid to the curb before a large building flaunting a sign to inform the public that within were beautiful one-room pullman kitchenette apartments for rent. The desk clerk in the imitation Spanish lobby informed us that Mr. Paige was expecting us, to go right up, apartment 94. Jerry Paige was waiting for us at the door of the automatic elevator when it stopped at the ninth floor. He was a long, slim young man with tawny gold hair and brown eyes.

"Inspector Daggett, I believe. The clerk rang and said you were on the way up, and— For the love of mud, Jim McBride! I didn't know you were in Chicago."

"You don't read the papers. I'm doing a signed column for the *Leader*, and living out in Oak Park with my mother."

"Sure, I've seen it, but didn't know it was you. Should have recognized the old touch, though."

"I've meant to look you up before. Wish I'd done it before I had to come with such bad news."

"It was good of you to come along now." The light of greeting died from his eyes as the reason for our visit was recalled. "But I don't understand all this. I'm still confused. Virtue called me but didn't have time to explain anything. Please come in and tell me just what happened last night."

Seated in the living room of the little furnished apartment Daggett told once again the story of the preceding night.

"It seems quite mad and perfectly inexplicable," Jerry said when the recital came to an end. "Uncle Jonathan was one of the kindest and most conservative men I have ever known. To have him meet his death in this horrible and fantastic manner seems incredible."

"Unfortunately, these are the facts," said Daggett. "Now will you please tell us your story of exactly what happened last night and omit nothing which could possibly have any bearing on your uncle's death? You were one of the last persons to see your uncle alive and anything you can remember about that last interview may be significant."

"That is true," he said slowly, "but I can't tell you much that is

31

helpful. Aunt Agatha called me day before yesterday at the hospital and asked me to come to dinner and go to the opera with them. I was to escort a girl named Vera Dawson, daughter of a friend of Aunt Agatha's. I'd never met her before, but she turned out to be a very nice girl. I went over to Astor Street to dinner last night about seven. It was a pleasant dinner party, just the Dawsons, myself and my aunt and uncle. Nothing unusual happened either there or at the opera."

"You noticed nothing out of the way in the manner of either your aunt or your uncle?"

"No. Uncle Jonathan didn't have much to say at dinner, but then he never does. He always leaves all the social end of things to Aunt Agatha and she carries things off efficiently by herself."

"And at the opera? Did your uncle receive any messages or talk to anyone outside your own party?"

"No one in particular. Uncle Jonathan and Miss Dawson and myself went out for a smoke between the acts and spoke to a few acquaintances, but just to pass the time of day. I don't remember Uncle having any real conversation with anyone."

"Do you know or have you ever heard your uncle speak of a man named Smeraldo?"

"No, why?"

Daggett drew a billfold from his pocket and extracted the crumpled notes signed Signor Smeraldo. "These were found in the pocket of your uncle's coat when Mr. McBride discovered him in the taxi. Do they mean anything to you?"

Paige read them through and then sat staring at them fixedly before he handed them back. "I have never heard of such a person and I have no idea how it came into my uncle's possession," he said firmly.

"Did your uncle meet anyone after the opera?"

"No, we went right out to his car which was waiting. The Dawsons had their own car. Uncle Jonathan asked me to drop in for a drink and a sandwich before I went home."

"What did you do then?"

"Aunt Agatha said she was tired and went right upstairs. Uncle and I went into the library and he opened the safe and got out his jewel collection. He has some very rare and beautiful pieces, you know, and he has just bought a bracelet of emeralds and pearls in enameled gold, supposed to have belonged to Catherine of Russia. He wanted me to see it. Uncle and I feel much the same about gems and beautiful workmanship."

"Yes," broke in Daggett. "What did you have to eat and drink?"

"Virtue brought in a plate of sandwiches and whiskey and soda."

"Did your uncle drink with you?"

"No, he very rarely takes any kind of alcoholic liquor. Doctor's orders, I believe."

"Did he say anything about some tonic he was taking?"

"Oh, yes, that green stuff. Dr. Bentley, the family physician, prescribed it for him after he had the flu early this fall. Uncle has taken it

32

before and swears by it when he is run down. It's some sort of harmless iron and sulphur mixture, I think. He took the bottle from the drawer of his desk, poured it out in the glass Virtue had brought and said something about it being his evening libation and he'd better not mix his drinks."

"Do you recall whether or not he drank it while you were in the room with him?"

"No, I don't believe he did. He poured it out and stowed the bottle away and then began opening up his cases of jewels to show them to me. I drank my highball while he was telling me the history of his new piece, but I think his medicine was still sitting untouched on the tray when I went out. I couldn't be sure of that because I wasn't noticing particularly, of course. Why do you ask?"

"I want a complete picture of the evening with all details," said Daggett. Then changing the subject, he asked, "Did your uncle say anything about expecting another visitor later in the evening?"

"No, he told Virtue not to wait, said he'd lock up when I went."

"Have you ever heard of a Madame Emeraude?"

"No, who is she?"

"That's what we'd like to know. A woman who was registered at the Congress Hotel as Madame Emeraude from Versailles called upon your uncle last night after you had left. He answered the door himself; she was with him about half an hour. Then he escorted her back to her hotel in her own taxi which was waiting. He took another taxi at the hotel and rode out to Oak Park to Mr. McBride's apartment as I explained. The woman left the hotel early this morning. We know only that she was young, pretty, blond, and dressed in black. Can you give us any clue as to who she might be?"

Paige hesitated, and when he answered, I noticed that his eyes were averted behind his golden lashes though his voice was straightforward enough. "None at all. My uncle had no women friends, that I know of," he said finally. "He is rather shy with pretty young women. I can't conceive of his doing such a thing, but then, one never knows."

"He didn't speak to a blond woman in black velvet at the opera?"

"No." Again there was an opaque look in his eyes that puzzled me.

"Have you been in the habit of going often to your uncle's house?"

"No. I'm invited to dinner there about once a month, and I never go unless I'm invited specially. Aunt Agatha isn't the sort one drops in on casually. I meet Uncle downtown for lunch quite often. Had lunch with him at the Union League last Monday."

"Are you on good terms with your aunt?"

"Oh, yes; she's always friendly and polite. I've always resented the fact that she's tried to prevent any intimacy between Uncle and myself. She cuts him off from lots of things and I've never felt she gave him much in return."

"You think they were not happy together?"

"Oh, I wouldn't say that. Everything was all right and they were always amiable enough in their relations with each other, which is more than lots of married people are able to do. I still cherish illusions about marriage though. I'd expect more than that and I'd like Uncle to have a little more appreciation."

"They were married abroad, I believe. Is your aunt a foreigner?"

"No, she is an American. She had married an Italian; Juliano Montebruzzi, his name was, a broken-down count of some sort whom she'd met when she was traveling abroad with her mother. Aunt Agatha was a lovely golden-haired widow living in a crumbled villa in Florence when Uncle met her. He married her and brought her back with him. It was a rather sudden courtship. He'd only known her a few weeks. He's not an impetuous man as a rule, though he does have queer romantic notions at times."

"Do you think it possible that your uncle could have taken his own life?" asked Daggett.

"I can't believe it. He was a very cheerful old boy, happy in his quiet way and healthier than he looked because he was so dried up. He was a bit frail, had to be careful of his heart, but he didn't suffer at all and wasn't worried about his health. I thought he was in unusually good spirits last night."

"Did he have financal worries?"

"Oh, he's lost a good deal of money in the last few years, but his business is sound. He can't lay his hands on cash as easily as he could ten years ago, but that certainly wouldn't drive him to suicide."

"He can't raise enough cash to buy you a practice in Evanston, is that it?"

Jerry winced. "Oh, you know about that, do you?" he said angrily. "That was just a little private talk between the two of us. I had had an opportunity and put it up to Uncle. He felt he couldn't swing it for me at present. That's all."

"Thank you, Mr. Paige. I must be off now. Where can I reach you if I need to get in touch with your during the day?"

"I'll be at the hospital all afternoon and early evening, unless I'm needed on Astor Street, which I doubt. I'm going over there now as soon as I can fix myself a cup of coffee. Virtue's call woke me and I haven't had time for any breakfast yet. Can I offer either of you a cup of coffee?"

"Thank you, no," said Daggett.

"I was planning to stop at Thompson's and get myself one, but I'd rather share the pot with you, Jerry, if you'd like me to," I said.

"I would, surest thing you know," said Jerry in heartfelt tones. I knew the kid was depressed and wanted company, and also there was a possibility that he'd say things to me alone that he wouldn't let out with Daggett present.

The inspector departed with a rather puzzled backward glance at me. Jerry plugged in his percolator and began to lay the table in his little dinette. I took on the job of making some toast.

"I haven't had a chance to tell you how bad I feel about this, old-timer," I said, as I flipped the bread in the rack. "He must have been

34

a fine old fellow. I knew he was a good sort when I first saw him last night and was sorry that I'd never have an opportunity to get acquainted. And that was before I had any idea who he was."

"Thanks, Jim. It certainly was a coincidence, his arriving at your house last night. But if a stranger had to find him in that horrible way, I'm damned glad it was you. He was the best friend I had in the world. We were together last night, and this morning he's gone. That inspector thinks I had a hand in it. Doesn't he, Jim?"

"He's not suspecting anyone at present. He hasn't got enough to go on," I replied gently. "But it's nasty business, buddy, and you'd better watch your step. You didn't do it, did you?"

"God, no!"

"Well, don't hold anything back then. It will only get you into trouble. You have something on your mind now that you haven't told."

"You always were an observing devil, Jim. What makes you think that?"

"I noticed the way you hid behind your eyelashes when he was talking about Madame Emeraude, the blond lady in black."

"I did nothing of the sort, you idiot. But to tell the truth, his questions did remind me of something that happened last night, but there didn't seem to be any real connection, so I didn't mention it. I told the truth right enough. I've never heard of Madame Emeraude and Uncle doesn't go in for blondes. I don't myself as a rule, but there was a girl who sat in the box next to us last night, a fair girl in black velvet alone. She popped into my mind when Daggett was talking, but none of us knew this girl; there was nothing really to identify her with this other blonde, and she was so lovely that I hated to drag her into this mess even by mentioning her."

"What was she like?"

"Like a freesia."

"You'd better elucidate. I never was any good at botany."

"Well, the first thing I noticed was the back of her head as she was sitting in the box. I saw a thick coil of silky hair, silvery in the shadow and gold where it caught the light. I'd never seen any hair quite like it. Then while I was staring, she turned around and almost floored me with a limpid look from the biggest, most luminous green eyes I've ever seen. They were like pools of clear green water, and her skin was like freesia petals. I could almost smell their fragrance as I looked at her. But this is stupid drivel at a time like this. I didn't mean to wax so poetic."

"She sounds well worthy of it. What was she wearing?"

"A black velvet dress, very simply cut and clinging, and she had a charming figure. But the most striking part of her toilette was her necklace, the only jewel she wore. The necklace itself was a sort of network of beautifully wrought pale gold chain set with small emeralds and diamonds so that the whole thing shimmered like falling water in the sunlight. At the end of the chain was an enormous carve emerald, the most scintillating and gorgeous stone I have ever seen. Even Uncle

35

nearly fell out of the box trying to get a good view of it. He said they were genuine stones, and he should know. Emeralds are his specialty."

"Your uncle did not speak to this woman or appear to recognize her?"

"No, we all looked at her a good deal, more than was polite I'm afraid. But so did almost everyone else. She created quite a sensation; a very beautiful and unusual woman alone in a box and wearing a dazzling jewel like that, she was bound to cause excitement. A number of people were asking about her but no one seemed to know who she was and she didn't go out between the acts or speak to anyone."

"Did she seem to be enjoying the sensation she had caused?"

"Well, no, she didn't. I thought she appeared rather shy and nervous. I admit I tried several times to catch her eye myself and get a smile, but I never succeeded. The woman has been pretty much in my mind ever since I first saw her. She's the kind one does not forget. You don't think she can be the one Daggett is after, do you?"

"Can't say, old-timer," I said guardedly. I was thinking of Pierre's gesticulating hands as he said, "*des yeux*—green they seemed but perhaps only because she wear the green *bijoux*." "Did you see her leave the opera house?" I asked.

"No, we left a few minutes early to avoid the rush and I didn't see her again. Toward the end of the last act the usher came into her box and handed her something, a note I think it was. She read it through quickly and seemed rather worried over it and uncertain what to do."

"Did your uncle see her get this note?"

"No, I don't think so. As a matter of fact, I'm afraid that he had dozed off a bit about then; he's apt to do that at the opera. I think I was the only one who noticed what went on in the next box. Miss Dawson and Aunt Agatha were intent on the stage, but I confess I watched the girl more than I did the singers."

"Could you identify her if you saw her again?"

"Oh, yes. I suppose you're going to pass this on to Daggett, aren't you? I sort of forgot that you were a newspaperman who was lucky enough to have a headliner story arrive at his front door. Are you being a detective in this case too?"

"I admit it was a scoop for me, old-timer, and Daggett is a good friend of mine. But no one could wish more devoutly than I do that Jonathan Crane was sitting in that nice library of his gloating over his emeralds right now. In helping Daggett I'm devoting myself to his cause and to yours. And frankly, I'm inclined to think that before this is over, you are going to be more anxious than anyone to locate this woman with the green eyes. If she is Madame Emeraude, she saw your uncle after you did, and knows why he went on that last ride to Oak Park."

"I didn't mean to be huffy," said Jerry miserably. "God knows I want the person who did for Uncle Jonathan brought to justice, and I also have sense enough to realize that I may need a friend badly before we're through with this. What a horrible tangle it all is!"

"I wish I knew why Crane gave the driver that Oak Park address. He had no friends nor even business connections out there, so far as we have been able to discover. The fact that you and I are friends is the only possible link."

"You mean that you think I sent him out there? That because I said I was glad that you were the one to find him that I planned it that way? That I poisoned him and then sent him off to you? I didn't know you lived in Oak Park. Why, in heaven's name—"

"No, no, I didn't mean that," I interposed hastily, though it had occurred to me that Daggett might have made some such interpretation when he found that Jerry and I were old friends. "Probably that green-eyed girl lives in Oak Park. She's hardly the type, but you never can tell. Well, I must be shoving off."

"Jim!" cried Jerry with sudden urgency in his voice. "You're on the inside of this. You'll let me know what is happening. I feel so in the dark, so helpless. Daggett thinks I did it. I could tell. I feel hemmed in by suspicions, I don't know what I ought to do."

"You can count on me, old-timer, but don't forget you're on the inside too, plenty, and you've got to co-operate. No holding out on anything."

"Okay. It's a partnership then?"

"Sure. Thanks for the breakfast and I'll be seeing you."

CHAPTER 6

AFTER I left Jerry's, I dropped in at Daggett's office.

"Well," he said, "did you get anything more out of young Paige over that cup of coffee you stayed for?"

"Sure," I replied. "I discovered that Madame Emeraude occupied the box next to the Cranes' at the opera last night. Jerry gave me a description of her that tallies perfectly with that of Pierre and the desk clerk, except that it was more floral and effusive. He was especially impressed with an emerald necklace which she was wearing. You remember Pierre mentioned *le bijou* which made her eyes look green." And I went on to recount all the details about the green-eyed girl which Jerry had given me.

"She ought not to be hard to locate if she makes as much impression as that on every man who sees her."

"What's new down here?"

"The chemist's report has come in. The medicine bottle is okay. Contains nothing except the tonic. We checked up with Dr. Bentley who prescribed it and the drug clerk who put it up identified the bottle and his own writing on the date on the label. The sandwiches were harmless too and the whiskey glass, but the sticky green stuff in the bottom of the medicine glass showed definite traces of strophanthus. The poison must have been put into the glass after Crane poured the medicine from the bottle. Both Virtue and Paige said that he poured it out himself."

"That means the poisoner must have had access to the room between the time that Crane poured out his medicine and the time he drank it, whenever that was. The effects are not immediate and the chemist said that the dose was not heavy. If Crane hadn't been a rather frail old man with a weak heart, it might not have put him out completely."

"How about the fingerprints?" I asked.

"No clear ones on the bottle except Crane's. Crane's and one other set on the glass. I presume the others are Virtue's, since he brought the glass in, but we haven't got his prints yet. The prints on the whiskey glass are a different set, undoubtedly Paige's. We'll get his later. I'm sending a man over to his apartment."

"You've picked Jerry as the main suspect, I take it."

"Well, he had both motive and opportunity. He needs money and undoubtedly stands to benefit by his uncle's will. He admitted that he knew of his uncle's habit of taking a tonic before retiring. He has access to a hospital laboratory and drug supply where he could easily have got the poison. He told us himself that his uncle poured out the tonic and left it on the table while they looked at the jewels. What could be simpler than for Paige to drop something into it while they are looking at those velvet cases? And if the old boy had gone on up to bed, his death would probably have been attributed to heart failure and none of this trouble would have occurred for the poisoner."

"But Jerry says the old man didn't drink that tonic while he was with him. That leaves the way open for others."

"Well, naturally he would say that. If we could prove he drank it while Jerry was there, the case would be clinched."

"But we can't, so that lady caller who arrived just after Jerry's departure had just as good an opportunity."

"Yes, but how could she know that there would be a liquid handy to drop her deadly potion into?"

"A charming lady can always say she's thirsty and then refuse prettily to drink alone."

"True."

"And how about Virtue? I suspect a man with such a name. He knew his master's habits and could have dropped something into the tonic easily enough. Nobody pays any attention to the hoverings of a butler; he's just part of the scenery."

"Then there are those footprints outside the French doors."

"Of course, the man on the balcony. We aren't sure whether he came into the room or not, but if he did, it must have been furtively. If he'd had legitimate business with Crane, he'd have used the front door instead of climbing over iron railings and peering in windows."

"If he poured the poison into the medicine glass, Crane must have seen him."

"He could have popped in, when Crane went to answer the door."

"That would have been quick work, but it's possible, I suppose."

"And how about Mrs. Crane? She's scared of something, behind that frigid assurance of hers. Maybe she came downstairs, found her husband in a tête-à-tête with this green eyed paragon and filled up his tonic with a death potion in a fit of jealousy."

"It could hardly have been a mood of the moment, since ladies don't go around equipped with vials of posion as a general thing."

"Well, perhaps she sent Violet back for it. And how about Violet? I think there are secret depths to that girl's heart. She'll bear watching."

"You watch her then," said Daggett impatiently; "I have more important things to do. Of course, anyone in the house could have managed it, even old Bruns."

"How are you coming with your investigation of Crane's activities? He seems to have been a livelier old gent than his family gave him credit for."

"I've had an interview with his secretary, Miss Elizabeth Cotton. Got one pretty hot tip. It seems that Crane went out to keep a mysterious appointment last Saturday about 10:30. Miss Cotton usually has complete information about all his appointments, but he wouldn't tell her anything about this.

"The appointment was made by phone the previous afternoon. A man called—Miss Cotton said the name was Schmidt or Schultz or something like that—and he had a German accent. She put the call through to Mr. Crane and didn't hear anything more of the conversation. Afterwards Crane told Miss Cotton to cancel another appointment he had made for Saturday morning as he had something more important to do at 10:30. He seemed sort of excited and puzzled, she said.

"He kept the appointment and got back to the office a bit after twelve and told Miss Cotton that he had to raise $20,000 in cash immediately. The banks were almost ready to close by that time, but he went right to work to see about selling some securities and on Tuesday morning he took the $20,000 in thousand-dollar bills from the First National Bank. We have the numbers listed. He left his office about 10 o'clock Tuesday morning, went to the bank and drew this money and didn't return until about 2 o'clock. Miss Cotton has no idea where he went or what he did with the money."

"Perhaps he was buying more jewels."

"I'd thought of that. Miss Cotton said she would call all the firms with whom he usually had dealings and ask if he had made any purchases in the last few days or if they had anyone named Schmidt or Schultz on their staff. I haven't heard from her, so apparently she has drawn a blank."

"Miss Cotton isn't a green-eyed blond, is she?"

"No, she has gray hair and brown eyes and has been with Crane for fifteen years."

"Well, I've got to get back to the office and pound out some sort of a column." I knew I had to watch my step if I was going to stay on the inside track with Daggett and didn't want to be too much underfoot.

Back at the office I was nabbed by a couple of cub reporters before I could get to work. I said I had a deadline to meet and managed to shake them off, and sat down to the old machine without an idea in my head.

I had just ripped out the last page of one of the sloppiest little pieces I've ever written, when I noticed a small figure standing tense and wide-eyed at the corner of my desk, a boy of about twelve, with his cap in his hand and his gaze fixed upon me. He'd apparently slipped in without my notice and had been watching me for several minutes, aware by some instinct that small boys don't interrupt newspapermen writing against a deadline.

"Hello, sonny," said I. "What are you doing here? Come down to see how a newspaper is made?"

"No, sir, not exactly. That is, I think newspaper offices are awful exciting and I'm going to be an editor when I grow up, but that isn't why I came down here."

"No? Well, what's on your mind?"

"Well, you see, I read your column every day and I like it fine and I've always wanted to meet you."

"Thanks a lot," I said, "but I'm pretty busy today. Is that all you wanted to see me about?"

"Well, no. You see, when I read about how it was you that found Mr. Jonathan Crane in that taxicab last night, why I remembered something that I'd heard about Mr. Crane and I thought maybe you'd be a good person to tell it to."

"I'm a fine person to tell things to," I replied. "What's your name?"

"Tommy McCarty; I'm Irish too." He grinned.

"Good, we Irish must stick together. Now what do you know about Mr. Crane?"

"I don't know Mr. Crane himself; I just heard somebody talking about him the other night."

"Yes, and what did they say that you thought would interest me?"

"Well, I live over on North Clark Street in an apartment over Schultz's antique and novelty store. Mr. Schultz has his shop on the first floor and he lives on the second floor and my mother and my sister and me live on the top floor. Schultz is a funny old German fellow, but he's awful interesting and he's been all over the world and he lets me come down and talk to him evenings. He explains all about the funny things in his shop and tells me about his pictures. He's got some swell stuff."

"I don't doubt it, but how about getting to the point? I'm busy."

The kid looked at me reproachfully. "I had to explain about Schultz because he's the one who was talking about Mr. Crane. You see, I went down there a couple of nights ago and there was another man there, a man with a black beard named Rakowitz that is a friend of Schultz's. Schultz is sort of used to having me around, so he didn't pay no mind to me, but just went on talking to Rakowitz. He was asking his advice about what he should do with a piece of jewelry he had. Some Italian guy had brought it in and asked him to sell it on commission. Schultz didn't want to take it, 'cause it was a much more valuable piece than he is used to handling and he told the fellow that he'd better take it to one of the big jewelers in the Loop. This guy didn't want to do that and he told Schultz that there was a man named Crane over on Astor Street who collected old jewelry and was specially interested in emeralds and he suggested that Schultz call him and get him to come over and look at this piece. It seems the Italian was too high and mighty to soil his hands with barter; that's what Schultz said."

"Did you say this jewel was an emerald?"

"Yeah, this guy said it had been in his family for a couple of generations, and he would never part with it except on account of needing some money right away."

"Do you know what the Italian's name is?"

"Yeah, his name is Ben Pirani. He has a room over on La Salle Street. I think Schultz has sold some other junk for him. Well, anyway, Rakowitz was telling Schultz he was a fool not to try selling it and get the commission, even if it wasn't in his line. He told Schultz he'd heard of Crane and thought it was just the sort of thing he'd be interested in. Schultz said he guessed he was right and he'd call Crane in the morning. Then they started arguing about Hitler and I went home."

"When was all this?"

"Last Thursday night."

"Have you seen this emerald, Tommy?"

"Not that night, but Pirani had left it in Schultz's safe and next day he called Crane and Crane came over Saturday morning and said he'd get the money the first of the week. I was down in the shop Saturday night. Schultz was alone and I asked him about the necklace and teased him to let me see it. He didn't want to get it out at first. I guess he was kind of worried about having it around, but he finally opened the safe and got it out for me. Gee, it certainly was swell!"

"Can you describe it?"

"It was a great big emerald with sort of designs in it, and it was hung on a lacy network of gold chain all set with little diamonds and emeralds. It all just sparkled and shimmered. You just had oughta see it, Mr. McBride."

"You're quite right, Tommy," I agreed; "I ought to see it. And you're going to take me right now."

Tommy climbed proudly into a taxi with me and gave the address to the driver with an air of pleased importance. We alighted before a dingy little shop which bore the sign, "Aug. Schultz, Antiques and Art Goods." There was no one in sight when we entered and as Tommy led me down the cluttered aisle, I had time to observe that Mr. Schultz's stock was a strange mixture of cheap novelty art ware and really fine old pieces of furniture and bric-a-brac. Presently Schultz, a rotund little German, came waddling up with a broad smile for Tommy and a

41

courteously inquiring look for me.

"This is Mr. McBride," began Tommy. "He came over to—"

I gave Tommy a warning nudge and interrupted with, "I've heard a great deal about your interesting shop, Mr. Schultz, and Tommy said you wouldn't mind if I came in to look around."

"Indeed, yes, glad to have you. Anything in particular you'd like to see?"

"That is a very interesting picture there, Mr. Schultz. Might I ask who the artist is?"

"Your humble servant, sir," replied Schultz with a little bow, beaming upon a lurid representation of the Castle of Chillon by moonlight. "One of my most recent. In fact the paint is hardly dry."

"Really. You handle jewelry also, don't you, Mr. Schultz?"

"Oh, yes, I have a few nice pieces. What you like? Rings, bracelets?"

"My young friend here was telling me that you have a very handsome emerald necklace."

"So, about my emerald necklace you have been talking, eh, Tommy?" said Shultz, fixing the boy with a round reproachful eye.

"I know you told me not to blab about it, Mr. Schultz, but you said that was just because you didn't want people to know that you had anything so valuable in your safe. But Mr. McBride—"

"Don't fret, *mein kind*, it makes no difference now because I sold the necklace yesterday."

"I'm sorry," I said, concealing my inner excitement at this announcement. "I should like to have seen it. Would you mind telling me the name of the purchaser?"

"He asked most particular that the sale be kept secret. I'm afraid I can't give you his name," said Schultz nervously.

"Mr. Schultz, do you read the newspapers?"

"I read the *Zeitung* but I don't like these American newspapers with their murders and divorces all over the front page. I only take a city paper to keep track of the auction sales and art exhibits."

"Evidently, then, you have not read any of the newspaper accounts in the morning papers of the death of Jonathan Crane."

Schultz's brown eyes bulged with horror and astonishment. "Jonathan Crane. But, no! It was only yesterday that— But when did this happen?"

"He was found dead last night in a taxicab. He died as a result of poisoning. I wonder if you can tell us anything about his activities of yesterday."

"You have guessed right. It was Crane who bought the emerald. He asked me not to tell anyone, because his collection is well known and he didn't want any publicity about the purchase. He didn't give me his reasons. But, of course, this is different. Poisoned, you say? Do you mean he was murdered?"

"Murder it is, Mr. Schultz, and I am sure you will be willing to give us any information you can that may help in tracking his murderer."

"*Ach, du lieber,* I knew that green stone would bring me bad luck.

42

I never wanted to have anything to do with it. Did they murder Mr. Crane for the emerald?"

"I don't know. Who do you mean by 'they'?"

"The people who murdered him. Oh, me, oh my, I'm very much upset. Are you a detective?"

"Not exactly, but I'm working on the case."

"Well, come into my back room where we can be private and I'll tell you what I can about it. Dear, dear, and such a nice gentleman he was, too!"

Schultz led us into a stuffy little parlor at the back of the shop.

"Suppose you start at the beginning, Mr. Schultz, and tell me how you got the necklace."

"This young Italian named Benedetto Pirani brought it in. He moved into this neighborhood a couple of weeks ago and took to dropping into the shop to talk to me. He told me that he belongs to a titled Italian family and I don't think he's lying because he has nice manners and knows French and German. I sold one other piece for him, a gold and enamel snuff box, beautiful thing, genuine eighteenth century, that he said had been in his family for generations, but he needed some cash and I got a client over on the Gold Coast who is collecting snuff boxes so I knew I could place it right away. I sold it for $500, as big a sale as I ever made here until Ben made me sell his emerald. *Ach*, was I dazzled the day he came in here with that necklace in a velvet case and asked me to sell it for him! I told him first that I couldn't do it and I should have stuck to my word.

"It was an unusual stone, not perfect, but unusually large and brilliant and there were some queer carvings on it. Ben said it was Russian workmanship. It was hung on a chain, sort of a netted thing of hand-wrought gold links set with chip diamonds and emeralds that gave a very glinting, beautiful effect, like shimmering water. Ben said it had been in his family for two hundred years and he hated to part with it. He said that there was an old superstition that the family always met with bad luck as soon as the emerald went out of their possession. But he was too desperate for money to pay any attention to family traditions, he said. He asked if I thought I could sell it for him? I told him right away that he'd better take it to some big jeweler in the Loop because I couldn't think of buying it outright and there was no one among my clients who would be likely to buy anything so expensive. He wanted spot cash for it too, he said.

"He didn't want to take it to the city, I don't know why. He said he'd heard of a man who lived over on the Gold Coast who had a collection of jewels and was particularly interested in emeralds. He was willing to let the necklace go for less than it was worth in order to get cash immediately and he was sure this man would be interested. I asked him why he didn't take it to the man himself and he said that he had never tried selling anything and he was sure he would be swindled. Besides, it was enough of a blow to his pride to let the emerald go at all without playing huckster for it himself yet. I said I'd think

43

it over, and he left the emerald in my safe.

"Frankly, I didn't like the idea of his trying to sell such a valuable piece through an obscure shop like mine. I don't like to run any chances of being hauled up as a fence. I get plenty chances to do that sort of thing around here, you know, Mr. McBride, and I have to be careful. Jake Rakowitz happened to drop in to see me that night. He was asking me about my business and I told him about the emerald and showed it to him. He had heard of this man that Ben suggested as a purchaser—Jonathan Crane, it was—and he said he thought I was foolish not to try for a good commission while I had a chance. Ben's story seemed straight enough and I hadn't had any trouble with the snuff box, so next day I called Mr. Crane at his office."

"Do you remember what day it was that you called Crane?"

"It was last Friday. He seemed interested right away and made an appointment to come to my shop to see the emerald on Saturday morning. He came in about eleven o'clock and I could tell as soon as he set eyes on the necklace that he was excited about it and wanted it. Ben said he'd take $20,000 cash for it, though it was worth more than that. It seemed like a lot to me, but it was a bargain for that emerald and Mr. Crane didn't haggle about it at all. I told him that the owner wanted spot cash if he sold it at that price. Crane said that that was a bit awkward for him just now but that I should hold the necklace for him for a few days until he could raise the money. Tuesday morning he just calmly walked in with the $20,000 in thousand dollar notes in his wallet. I opened my safe and got out the emerald. He took it out of the case and held it up to the light, played with it a bit, then handed me the money. Then he put the necklace back in its case, dropped it into his pocket, and walked out, just like that yet, as if he'd bought a handkerchief or a pair of gloves. It was the quickest and easiest sale I ever made, as well as the biggest. But now the beautiful green stone has brought trouble, as I was always afraid it would. Ben's family curse, maybe. Where is the necklace now?"

"I don't know. You see, we didn't know that Mr. Crane had made this purchase until just now."

I tried to speak casually, but in my mind was an excited vision of a fair-haired slender girl in black velvet, seated alone in a box at the opera with a great emerald gleaming on her breast. What did this all mean? Was it just the usual story of an old man buying sparklers for his sweetie or was there something sinister and strange behind it all?

"Did Crane drop any hint as to whom he intended to give the jewel, or for what purpose he wanted it?" I asked.

"He just said he had a collection of jewels. He described some of them to me and told me he'd have me over sometime and show me the lot. I was very pleased and he promised to send for me. Now I can never go."

"Perhaps it can still be arranged for you to see the collection sometime. But why did Crane pledge you to secrecy about his purchase?"

"I don't know quite. He just said that his collection was well known; other dealers and collectors were interested in any additions he made

44

to it and he didn't want this purchase to be general knowledge. He didn't say why. Maybe he was afraid of being robbed, though you'd hardly think so from the pleased and careless way he dropped a $20,000 necklace into his pocket and walked off."

"Does anyone beside yourself know of this?"

"Not from me they don't. Of course, Pirani, he knows. He suggested Crane for buying it and besides, he says if he ever gets any money he's going to buy the emerald back. He thinks it brings him luck."

"What made Pirani think he could get it back from Crane? Collectors usually hang on to a piece that pleases them and won't give it up for love nor money."

"I don't know, but he seemed to think he'd get it back somehow."

"Have you turned the sum over to Pirani?"

"Yes, he was in that same morning, after Crane left. There were twenty thousand-dollar bills. I got one for my commission, handed over the other nineteen to him. I haven't seen him since."

"Where is the bill now?"

"It is in my safe still. I should have put it in the bank already, but I never had a thousand-dollar bill before and I wanted to show it to Rakowitz."

"Does Rakowitz know that you sold the necklace to Crane?"

"Yes, he dropped around last night for a chat and I told him all about it."

"What time was that?"

"Oh, early in the evening. He left here about 9:30."

"May I see the bill?"

"Sure, I'll get it for you."

Schultz heaved himself out of the sagging armchair and went into the shop, twirled the dial of the big black safe and returned carrying a crisp new banknote gingerly in his chubby fingers. I jotted down the number and handed it back to him.

"Have you any idea where Mr. Crane went when he left your shop?"

"Yesterday, you mean? No, he didn't say anything about going any place. He drove up in a taxi, but he didn't have it wait and I didn't see him hail another one."

"About what time was it when he left here?"

"About eleven-thirty."

"Can you give me Mr. Pirani's address?"

"Sure, it's a rooming house just around the corner and across the street. I'll write out the number for you." Schultz scrawled the address on a greasy card which he pulled from his pocket.

"Thank you, Mr. Schultz, you've been very obliging. If anything further should come up which you think might have any bearing on the case, I wish you would call me at the *Leader* office. Good morning, and again, thank you."

Tommy led me up the steep narrow stairs of an old brick house where he said Pirani lived. The slatternly woman who responded to my prolonged peal of the bell informed me, in reply to my inquiry, that Mr. Pirani had paid up his back rent just in time to prevent his being turned out on the pavement and had departed bag and baggage the day before. No, she didn't know where he had gone and didn't care. She had already rented the room to a good steady respectable auto mechanic from a Clark Street garage.

CHAPTER 7

DAGGETT was not in his office when I called to give him my latest discovery. The girl at the switchboard, after my pressing inquiry, said that he had gone over to Crane's office, so I hopped a cab to La Salle Street. A frizzle-headed little switchboard girl and a tall, lanky filing clerk with a straight black bang across her spectacled eyes were guarding the outer office, obviously thrilled and excited with happenings of the morning. After some persuasion the frizzlehead admitted that Daggett was in Mr. Crane's office with Miss Cotton and didn't wish to be disturbed.

"What's up?" said I.

The blonde looked coy, but the black bang was pining to talk.

"They found one of those thousand-dollar bills that Mr. Crane got from the bank yesterday. Somebody brought it into a Wilson Avenue bank and the bank called Miss Cotton."

"Well, you tell Miss Cotton there is a guy outside waiting to tell her where the other nineteen thousand-dollar bills are; name's McBride."

Frizzlehead looked at me goggle-eyed and then plugged in the call to the other office. Daggett and Miss Cotton were willing to see me, she discovered, and I marched over to the door marked "private" and closed it firmly against those two pairs of inquisitive eyes. Daggett was standing before the open office safe talking to a little woman with white hair and harassed brown eyes.

"This is Jim McBride," said Daggett, "an Irish newspaperman who has been following me around lately. What is your excuse for butting in now?"

I shook hands with Miss Cotton, ignoring Daggett's question, and then remarked that I'd heard one of the bills had been traced.

"We haven't traced it very far," growled Daggett. "A furrier named Jacob Rakowitz brought it into the Lakeshore Bank to be changed and fortunately the clerk checked on it and found it was one of the bills Crane had drawn yesterday. This bird said that he had sold a coat to a fellow, an Italian whose name he didn't know, who had paid for it with this bill. Sounds a bit fishy, but we may be on the trail of our friend Signor Smeraldo again."

"Sounds very fishy to me and though that fellow may call himself

Signor Smeraldo on occasion, is he known as Benedetto Pirani over on Clark Street."

"What are you talking about?" shouted Daggett and Miss Cotton's brown eyes popped very wide open.

"I've just been over at Pirani's rooming house looking for him, but he left bag and baggage yesterday and the landlady didn't know where he had gone."

"How do you think he got Crane's thousand-dollar bill?"

"He got nineteen of Crane's thousand-dollar bills, as a matter of fact, and the other one is in the safe of Augustus Schultz who has a shop on North Clark Street. He kept that one as his commission for selling Pirani's emerald necklace to Crane."

"What emerald necklace? Where did you get all this"

"From Schultz himself. I've just come from there."

"Who has the necklace now?"

"That's your problem, Daggett, you're the detective. Schultz turned it over to Crane yesterday morning in exchange for that twenty grand. He gave me a detailed description of it, but there was nothing like it among the jewels we saw this morning. But you remember that Pierre, the waiter, mentioned that Madame Emeraude was wearing green jewelry and the necklace which knocked Jerry's eye out on his beautiful lady in the opera box corresponds exactly to Schultz's description, a carved emerald on a netted chain of diamonds and emeralds."

"Well, I'll be damned!" muttered Daggett. "Have you ever heard him mention this emerald, Miss Cotton?"

"No, but it all fits in. That must have been Schultz who called him last week and I suspected he was buying gems because I could see that he was excited as only a new find for his collection can excite him. It is just like him to buy a jewel in that sudden offhand manner, particularly if he thought it was a bargain and didn't want to miss it by dickering around, but it isn't at all like him to give it away to a young lady."

"We've got to find that green-eyed dame," said Daggett grimly. "We needed her before, but this puts a different light on it. She certainly gave us the slip, but she's an eyeful according to all accounts and every precinct police station in Chi has a description of her now. She ought to be turning up soon."

"She was carrying a suitcase when last seen," I suggested helpfully; "maybe she's skipped town."

Daggett merely grunted. "Let's have this whole story about Schultz."

So I sat down and told the two of them everything I had learned in the little shop on Clark Street. "This Rakowitz who got Schultz into the business is undoubtedly the man who changed the bill. He was probably doing it as a favor to Pirani who is keeping under cover. I'll bet he knows where Pirani is, if you could get him to talk."

"I'll get him later; he'll keep. Did you get any line on where Crane had lunch yesterday, Miss Cotton?"

"No, I didn't. I had Stella call all of his regular places this morning and enquire, but no one had ever seen him. He must have eaten somewhere, because he has to be regular with his meals or he gets faint. He never skips lunch, and if he gave that girl the emerald, he must have met her around lunch time. He was in the office from three to six and went right home after that. I know because we took the same taxi and he got off first at his home."

"Schultz said that Crane didn't want him to mention the transaction to anyone and he'd promised not to. Apparently he was planning to make a gift of the stone and didn't want his wife to hear about it."

"He might have felt that way whether he was going to give it away or not," put in the secretary. "Mrs. Crane didn't approve of his putting so much money into his collection and you can hardly blame her. He had to sell good securities to raise the $20,000 and he was by no means so well able to afford such luxuries as he was in 1929. And of course, Mrs. Crane might not have objected so much if he had been buying the jewels for her, but he wouldn't even let her wear them."

"Do you know why?"

"Well, he never said much about it to me," replied Miss Cotton evasively, "but of course I knew him pretty well, working with him all these years, and I know how he felt about his gems. He regarded his collection as a complete and beautiful thing that shouldn't be broken up and used for personal display. Then, too, I think he used to identify his stones with certain characteristics and felt that jewels should match the character and appearance of the person who wore them.

"He told me once that when he first met Mrs. Crane in Italy—Contessa Montebruzzi she was then—she seemed a personification of some old gold and sapphire renaissance jewelry he had just bought. I've always had an idea that he got her mixed up in his mind with his jewels and brought her along as part of the collection. But I oughtn't to say such things.

"Well, anyway, he decided later that the Florentine jewelry didn't suit her as well as he had thought, even if it did match her coloring, so he took his engagement present back and locked it in the safe and bought her some platinum diamond engagement ring and a bracelet instead. I think she really prefers these modern smart things, but she understood him well enough to be insulted by this, and it has been a sore point between them ever since."

"Are you familiar with the terms of Mr. Crane's will?" broke in Daggett.

"There is a copy of it in the office safe. I imagine it would be all right for me to show it to you. The lawyer will be reading it tomorrow after the funeral anyway." Miss Cotton went to the safe and drew out a long envelope and handed it to Daggett, who opened it, drew out a legal blank and read:

Know all men, by these presents, that I, Jonathan Ebenezer Crane, of the city of Chicago, in the county of Cook, in the State of Illinois, being of sound mind and memory, do hereby make, publish and declare this my last will and testament, hereby revoking all former wills, bequests, and devises by me at any time heretofore made:

First: After the payment of my just debts and funeral expenses I give, devise and bequeath to my nephew, Gerald Crane Paige, my entire collection of gems, mounted and unmounted, and the sum of $50,000.

Second: To Rose Elizabeth Cotton, my secretary, I give, devise and bequeath the sum of $2,000.

Third: To John Virtue, my butler, I give, devise and bequeath the sum of $1,000.

Fourth: To my wife, Agatha Montebruzzi Crane, I give, devise and bequeath all other property, real and personal.

The will had been witnessed by Amos Binder and Stella Oppel and had been drawn up two years previously.

"Pretty handsome bequest to young Paige. That jewel collection must be worth a couple of hundred thousand and a nice bunch of cash thrown in," said Daggett. "I've heard that he is pretty hard up right now, too."

"Yes, I guess he is," affirmed the secretary.

"Do you know whether Paige was aware of the terms of the will?"

"I don't think so, though I wouldn't be sure. He would, of course, expect something on his uncle's death. As a matter of fact, Mr. Crane's fortune was considerably larger at the time the will was drawn up. Falling securities and the break in the market have made heavy losses for him. I know that he had considerable difficulty raising that $20,000. After Jerry's $50,000 is paid, I'm afraid the widow's estate will be rather small."

"This will was drawn up only two years ago and Mr. Crane has been married for six years. He must have made a will at that time. Do you know anything about the terms of it?"

"There was the same cash bequest to Jerry, but the jewel collection was left to his wife."

"Did Mrs. Crane know of this change in the disposition of the collection?"

"I don't think so, but of course I wouldn't know for sure."

"Thank you very much, Miss Cotton, for your frankness and helpfulness. I hope that you will continue to keep your eyes and ears open and report to me anything which may seem of any bearing on the case. You will keep the office open for a few weeks, at least, won't you?"

"Oh, yes, and I will be glad to help all I can. I was very fond of Mr. Crane and he was such a kind, considerate man to work for. I'll never find another employer as good."

"I have an appointment for another interview with Mrs. Crane," said Daggett as we left the office. "Paige said he would be at the Astor Street house this afternoon also."

"I want to see Jerry. I guess I'll go along," I said mildly.

"This friendship of yours with young Paige is sort of a break if your loyalties don't carry too far. You can get more out of him than anyone else, but are you willing to use any adverse material you find? I know of old how you'll stick by a friend, Jim."

"I'm for Jerry, of course, but if I came across proof that he'd poisoned a perfectly swell old uncle, he just wouldn't be the chap I took him for and bets would be off, savvy?"

The tall narrow house on Astor Street looked as austere and bleak in the late afternoon as it had on the early morning visit. Was it really only this morning that I had mounted those steps for the first time. It seemed like a week. The curtains were drawn across the windows; no lights were showing. A very solemn-faced Virtue answered the door.

"Mrs. Crane said that I was to show you up to her sitting room when you came. Mr. Paige is in the library," he announced.

"I'll go right up. Jim, you'd better go in and talk to Jerry."

Jerry's long, lean body was sprawled miserably in a big chair before the cold and empty fireplace, his feet on the gleaming brass fender.

"Hello," he said moodily. "Did Daggett come with you? I told him he could find me here this afternoon, so I had to stick around and wait for him, though I seem to be *persona non grata* in this house. Aunt Agatha refuses to see me at all, and Virtue coldly informed me that he had instructions to attend to all the funeral arrangements himself and would not need my assistance. Much more of this and I'll begin to think maybe I did dump some poison in the medicine glass, sort of absent-mindedly, you know. There have been detectives snooping around the hospital too, asking a lot of questions about me and poking in the laboratory. I've been doing some experiments there evenings on my own. Oh, yes, I could have got hold of strophanthus or any other kind of poison with no trouble at all. It is a very well equipped laboratory."

"That's all routine, you know. The police have to investigate," said I, moved to pity by the bitterness in Jerry's voice.

"They been prowling around my room too, going through my desk. The room clerk told me they had a warrant and he had to let them in."

"What would they find there?"

"Nothing much but a lot of unpaid bills, which would prove, of course, that I needed money and would poison my uncle as the most convenient way of acquiring it. I hope they didn't find any strophanthus in my kitchen cupboard, but the way I'm feeling at the moment I wouldn't even be sure of that."

"There is still Signor Smeraldo and Madame Emeraude. When we find that green-eyed woman, we'll have the clue to the tangle, I bet."

"I suppose I should be more keen than anyone else to have the cops get her, but somehow I dread having her dragged into this, having to identify her and everything."

"We've found out where she got that emerald she was wearing last night. Perhaps you will be able to overcome your reluctance at having to besmirch your beautiful freesia-lady when you hear how she came by that necklace you and your uncle admired so much."

50

"What do you mean?" cried Jerry.

I poured into his incredulous ears the story I had got from Schultz. This tale had not reached the Crane household as yet.

"Gosh, when Aunt Agatha hears that!" muttered Jerry. "But I don't understand it at all. It doesn't sound like Uncle Jonathan. I've never known him to chase a lady or give her presents."

"There was your Aunt Agatha in Florence, six years ago." I reminded him, "another beautiful blonde. Every six years isn't so often, you know."

"Just the same, I don't think she's a murderer," insisted Jerry. "I'm betting on the Italian, Smeraldo or Pirani or whatever you want to call him. He had an urgent reason for wanting to get the emerald back. He first tried to get in touch with the girl, knowing somehow that she had it—you remember the dark man who inquired for her at the hotel—followed her here that night, climbed up the balcony, slipped into the library when Uncle went to the door to let the girl in, and dropped poison into the medicine glass."

"Nice theory, but how did Pirani figure that poisoning Crane would get him the emerald? Ordinarily Crane would have drunk his medicine, gone to bed and been found dead in the morning. That, I'm quite sure, is what the poisoner intended. That ride to Oak Park spoiled the game. If it hadn't been for that, Crane's death might have passed for heart failure and none of this would have come to light. At any rate it is an odd way to go about a robbery."

"I know, but I'll wager the emerald is at the bottom of the whole thing and the person who has the necklace now is the one who murdered my uncle, and I think it is Pirani."

"Maybe so," said I. "But remember the green-eyed girl was wearing it when last seen and there's no reason to believe it has changed hands. Don't make a sentimental idiot of yourself over a woman you know nothing about really."

Just then the telephone on the big desk jangled. Jerry slumped back in his chair before the firepace, but I rose and went toward the desk.

"The servants will answer," said Jerry. "There are two other phones in the house."

Nevertheless, I went to the phone, but did not answer the call however as I heard Violet's voice already on the wire.

"Yes, Mrs. Crane is in," I heard her saying, "but she has a caller and gave orders that she was not to be disturbed. Can I take a message? This is Violet, her maid, speaking."

"Tell Mrs. Crane that Rakowitz, the furrier, called," said a foreign-sounding voice. "Her coat is ready for a fitting. I would like to try it on tomorrow."

"I'm sure that Mrs. Crane would not be interested in having her coat fitted tomorrow," replied Violet haughtily. "Her husband's funeral takes place tomorrow afternoon."

"Will you please give her the message in any case?"

"Very well."

"Don't forget; it is important. She is expecting to hear from me and will be annoyed if she thinks I have forgotten."

"Yes, I'll tell her. Good-bye," said Violet and the phone clicked.

"I suppose it's part of your job to listen in on other people's phone calls," muttered Jerry, "but it seems like snooping to me. What did you find out?"

"Nothing much. It was your aunt's furrier calling to arrange a fitting tomorrow. Now that seems odd, for he must have known about a tragedy in the family of an important client. Furthermore, he said his name was Rakowitz, which is also the name of that friend of Schultz's who suggested that he get in touch with Crane about the emerald. This man had an accent, but it seemed like an Italian or a French accent. Kind of fishy."

"Did Aunt Agatha talk to him?"

"No, Violet said she wasn't to be disturbed and took the message. She seemed to think it was funny, too."

"Look in the phone book and see if there is a Rakowitz who is a furrier."

"Yes," I said, after thumbing through the pages of the big book on the desk. "Here it is. I'd say from the address it was a small shop in the Wilson Avenue neighborhood. Guess I'll give them a ring myself, since I've bothered to look up the number."

A girl's voice answered my call. Mr. Rakowitz was in, would I hold the line a moment please.

"Yes, diss iss Rakowitz. Who iss speaking?" came a heavy voice over the wire.

I explained that I was Mr. Brown and wished to enquire what the charges would be for having earflaps added to my sealskin cap. I told him I found the price quoted satisfactory, and saying I would call soon with the cap, I hung up.

"Well," I said as I hung up the receiver, "unless he's produced an Italian son, that fellow who called before wasn't any Rakowitz. I'd like to know who he was."

"Probably just an assistant using his employer's name to save explanation," said Jerry.

"Maybe but I'd say this fur coat business would bear looking into. By the way, I'm thirsty. Think I'll go out to the kitchen and get a drink of water."

"Ring for Virtue. He'll get you one."

"I'd rather go myself. I know where the kitchen is," I said, and slipped quietly through the side door of the library which opened into the rear hall and the butler's pantry. The big kitchen was neat and empty. I drew a glass of water from the tap and stood drinking it and studying the pattern of the linoleum on the kitchen floor. The muddy tracks from the back door to the kitchen stairs had been wiped up and the whole floor was now clean and shining.

Suddenly there was a furious banging of the outer door, a swish of skirts and Violet burst into the kitchen, her hazel eyes flashing and unwonted spots of color in her smooth cheeks. She stopped short when she saw me, gave an embarrassed little laugh and tried to smooth her ruffled hair.

"What's the matter, Violet? Something chasing you out in the back yard?"

"No, sir, quite the contrary, I might say."

"You don't mean to say that anyone would be running away from a charming little girl like yourself?"

"Well, he just tells me cool as a cucumber that he can't take me out tonight when we'd been planning for over a week to go to the Aragon. And he doesn't even say he's sorry. Just goes on polishing the car, and doesn't even look at me, when just a few days ago— Oh, men are all alike! I'm going to quit this place, I am. What with detectives snooping around and the mistress cross as two sticks— Briscombe says it isn't respectful to go dancing when there's death in the house, but he could at least take me to the movies. I need to get away from here, I do. It's getting on my nerves."

"I'm not much of a dancer, Violet, but I know a nice little place on Superior Street where we can have a few good drinks and a nice little talk. How about it?"

"Okay. I can get away by eight-thirty, I think. It'll serve Briscombe jolly well right. Say, you aren't a detective, are you."

"Oh, no, I'm just a newspaper man and a friend of Mr. Paige."

"I don't want to have any drinks and little chats with any detectives. They're too nosey and you never know what they're going to make of what you say. But I liked you from the start and I've always thought Mr. Paige was a grand man. I'm crazy about men with those hot brown eyes. Briscombe has that kind, too, only his are darker than Mr. Paige's."

"I answered the telephone in the library this afternoon and heard you talking to a foreign gentleman, sounded like an Italian. Has he hot brown eyes too?"

"You're a fine one listening in on me. Answered the phone, did you? I didn't hear you helloing very loud."

"I heard you talking and hung up again," I said.

"Well, you wouldn't have heard anything if you hadn't. It was just Mrs. Crane's furrier calling about her coat. I thought at first I recognized the voice, but I must have been wrong."

"Who did you think it was?"

"Oh, just a fellow I met at a dance the other night. I thought maybe he was calling for a date and got quite a flutter."

"Did you know that Mrs. Crane was having her coat repaired?"

"Yes, she drove over there with it yesterday."

"Does she always have her fur work done with Rakowitz?"

"No, she's always gone to Marshall Field's before. I don't know who put her onto this place. She just had a rip in the sleeve. I don't see why she had to have a fitting."

"I must be going, Violet. I'll call for you here about eight-thirty."

"Right-o, I'll be ready."

"Well," said Jerry, when I sauntered back into the library, "it takes you a long time to get a drink of water."

"I got more than I planned on," I grinned. "A glass of water and a date."

CHAPTER 8

I LEFT the office late in the afternoon feeling very weary and deflated. I'd had no sleep the previous night, and I was hungry too. Then I remembered that earlier in the day I had thought of looking around at the eating places near Schultz's shop with the idea that perhaps Crane had lunched in the neighborhood. I'd called Schultz to ask him about the matter, and he had told me that there was a place called McGilvary's in the next block that was pretty good. I went over and clambered aboard a crowded Clark Street car; I'd already spent too much on taxis. I could get a meal at McGilvary's whether they had any information to get me or not, and stop in for a chat with Schultz after dinner. Then a few minutes' walk would take me from the clanging cars and junky shops of Clark Street over to the Gold Coast, the quiet dignity of Astor Street and the dubious charms of Violet.

Apparently McGilvary's patrons dined early, for the restaurant was already well filled when I arrived. I looked about for the proprietor and decided that the tall man with the long thin nose, closely placed eyes and graying sandy hair must be McGilvary. He looked rather like a Scotch collie. However, he was busy distributing menus, greeting his patrons as they entered, and speeding the waitresses along with their heavy trays. Feeling that it would be wiser to save my questions until the rush hour was over and I had proved myself an honest customer, I scanned the tables with their red checked cloths and saw one vacant at the back of the room near the swinging door to the kitchen.

The menu, with the exception of Scotch shortbread and oatcakes, as a tribute to McGilvary's highland ancestors, was typical of the American beanery. I decided that a T-bone steak and mashed potatoes would be as safe as anything and looked about for my waitress. She was gathering up the gravy-smeared plates at the next table, preparatory to bringing in the pie. Nice blond hair and remarkably good figure, I thought idly, as I watched her pile the dishes on a big tray. Quite pretty, too, I saw, as she moved around to the other side of the table so that I could see her face bent over the cluttered plates, though she was a bit white and tired-looking. Long hours and many heavy trays; a place like this must be hard on a girl. She piled the last side dishes of creamed corn with the butter plates; now her tray was full, she straightened herself for the effort of gathering up its weight and sent a little apologetic glance over to where I was sitting, just one little direct glance to say, "Sorry to keep you waiting, I'll come as soon as I can." Then she hoisted the heavy tray on the flat of one hand and steadying it with the other, hurried past me and through the swinging doors to the kitchen.

However, that one look was enough to make my heart pound with excitement and my hands grip convulsively so that the neatly typed menu crumpled to a ball in my grasp. For the eyes that had sent me that faint little apologetic glance had been green, green as emeralds in a face that was delicately oval and white as a freesia. I was acting foolishly, no doubt. There were lots of green-eyed women. I had had only that one glance from her eyes. Perhaps they had only looked green because of my present obsession. But no, there she was standing over the table, waiting for my order. Her eyes were undeniably green, translucent green grapes, and how white she was. She ought not to carry those heavy trays. And that soft hair, gold in the shadow and silver in the light—could there be two like that?

"Your order, please," she said very coolly and I realized that I had been staring at her and that she was repeating her request.

"I'm sorry," I said. "I'm waiting for a friend who was to meet me here. I think I won't order until he comes. Do you mind if I telephone and see what's keeping him?"

She looked at me rather strangely. "You can use the phone at the cashier's desk," she said, and turned back to the kitchen.

I hurried over to the desk, got the genial permission of the ringleted cashier for the use of the phone and gave the number of Jerry's apartment. To my great relief, he answered promptly.

"Jim McBride, Jerry. Have you had dinner?"

"Oh, hello, Jim. No. I'm eating here at the apartment; just put the chops on now. Why?"

"Can you put the grub back in the icebox and come over to Clark Street and have dinner with me?"

"Thanks," said Jerry, sounding a bit puzzled, "but I've got stuff already cooking and it's such a beast of a night to go out. Why don't you come on over and eat with me, I think I have enough for the two of us."

"I've already had breakfast at your place. I don't want to be a regular boarder. You come over to McGilvary's at — North Clark Street."

"What sort of a dump is McGilvary's? What's the idea?"

"I can't explain now. Get here as fast as you can," I said in an urgent tone, dropping the casual manner I had assumed for the benefit of the cashier.

"I'll be there," answered Jerry crisply and the phone clicked.

I lingered at the counter and bought a package of cigarettes and a newspaper which bore a flaring headline: "Mystery Woman Wears Crane's Emerald to Opera before the Murder."

"Gee, that's the most exciting murder story we've had around here

55

for a long time, isn't it?" said the cashier. "I wonder if they'll ever find that Madame Emeraude. She must be a slick one."

"Yeah," I agreed, still stalling around in the front of the cafe. I noticed some round tin boxes of imported Scotch shortbread; it is a favorite confection of Mother's, so I bought a box of that too, and then, since I had no excuse to linger longer and Jerry had not appeared, I strolled back to the table and lit a cigarette.

I sat and smoked and tried to keep an eye on the green-eyed waitress without making her too much aware of my attention. She was busy at another table, but I fancied she was conscious of my scrutiny and she seemed nervous and weary.

An elderly gentleman with chin whiskers came in and sat down at the table next to mine. He was evidently an habitué, for the girl greeted him with a kindly but listless, "Good evening, Mr. McCartney. What will it be for you tonight?"

He ordered clam chowder and oatcakes and then said, "You've been looking a wee bit peaked lately, Celia." she smiled at him and shrugged her thin shoulders. When she returned with his order, I noticed that her hand was shaking.

"Tut, noo, you're not wont to do a thing like that," cried Mr. McCartney, as he mopped off with his napkin the drops of clam chowder which had fallen on his coat sleeve.

So, she had been here long enough so that the patrons knew her well, called her Celia and commented on her health. Somehow all of this didn't fit in with my conception of a murderess and a jewel thief. But why was she looking peaked and why was she spilling soup today when her hand as a rule was steady?

I wished Jerry would hurry. McGilvary and the other waitresses were beginning to cast curious looks at me and the crowd was thinning out. There was Jerry at last, standing irresolutely in the doorway scanning the tables. He came hurrying over as I lifted a hand.

"What in the name of time is the idea of all this?" he said, as he flung off his wet coat and joined me at the little red checkered table.

"I may have brought you out on a wild goose chase. If so, I apologize. But take a good look at our waitress when she comes in."

I heard the swinging doors creak and felt the warmth of the steamy, food-laden air of the kitchen. The green-eyed waitress was coming to serve us. My back being to the door, I could not see her enter, but I saw written on Jerry's face all that I wanted to know. His tawny brown eyes suddenly widened and darkened, and he half rose in his chair. Then with one swift movement he left the table just in time to catch in his arms the wilted figure of the blond waitress. She had fainted.

Only a few of the remaining diners noticed the event. The other waitresses stared curiously, and McGilvary came hurrying over looking much annoyed. The girl recovered quickly and her white face flooded with rose when she looked up into Jerry's eyes. She pushed him away and stood weakly leaning on a chairback for support.

"You'd better go home, Celia," said McGilvary, "and don't come

56

back tomorrow unless you feel better. I'm very sorry, gentlemen, that you should have been disturbed. I'll get another waitress to take your order. Miss Emory seems indisposed."

"Yes, she does," I said quickly, rising and pushing back my chair. "I have my car outside. I'd be very glad to see Miss Emory home."

"Do permit us, Miss Emory," seconded Jerry.

The girl said nothing and McGilvary looked at us in bewilderment. "But your dinner, gentlemen, it is late. One of the other girls can see Miss Emory home."

"We'll come to dinner some other time," said I. "Will you come with us, Miss Emory?"

To our surprise the girl nodded. "I'll get my coat," she said softly.

"You'd better stay here," I said, laying an arresting hand on her slim shoulder. Then I turned to the perplexed manager. "Will you ask someone to bring Miss Emory's things?"

Jerry helped the girl into the shabby black coat that one of the other waitresses produced from the kitchen. She pulled a felt hat over her bright hair, and amid the curious looks of the occupants of the restaurant we started for the door.

"You're forgetting your shortbread," said the girl with a queer little catch in her voice.

"So I am. Thanks for reminding me," I said, and made a dash back to the table.

Out on the sidewalk Jerry and I looked at each other rather sheepishly. What were we to do with her? "We'll have to look around a bit for my car. My chauffeur couldn't find a parking space in front. Oh, there he is. Hi, Yellow!"

"I thought it would be that kind," murmured the girl, but she got into the taxi and took her place between us with no remonstrance.

"Where do you live, Miss Emory?"

"At —— La Salle Street. Do you intend to take me there?"

"Well now, come to think of it, Jerry, what are our intentions? The taxi-driver is wondering, too."

"We'd like to have a little talk with you, Miss Emory," said Jerry with an unwonted gentleness in his voice. "Would you mind, if you're feeling well enough now, coming up to my apartment for a little while?"

Without waiting for her answer, I called the address to the driver.

"I'll plug in the percolator of coffee again and heat up the lamb chops and we may eat yet this evening," said Jerry.

The rest of the ride was made in silence, Jerry and I stealing occasional furtive glances at the still white face of the girl who sat between us. She did not speak again until we had deposited our hats and coats in Jerry's little dressing room and were warming up his half-prepared dinner in the "pullman" kitchenette.

"May I help?" she asked. Jerry showed her where the silver was kept and she deftly set the little gateleg table for three. Jerry and I were hungry and started at the lamb chops and peas hurriedly; the girl merely toyed miserably with the food on her plate and drank

57

black coffee while we ate.

"I've seen you before," said Jerry. "Do you remember where?"

"Yes."

"*Rigoletto* is a delightful opera, isn't it?"

"Very."

"You were looking very lovely yourself that night, and that was a marvelous emerald you were wearing."

The girl's face flamed. "You are just trying to torment me with this little comedy," she said passionately. "Why did you bring me here? What do you want of me?"

"Do you know who I am?"

"Yes, you are Gerald Paige, nephew of Jonathan Crane. And you, I suppose"—she turned to me—"are a detective."

"Not exactly," I replied. "Just James McBride, a newspaper columnist, though I'm doing a little sleuthing on the side. Have you heard of the Crane case?"

"I've read what there has been in the papers."

"We have reason to believe, Miss Emory," I went on formally, "that you are familiar with some aspects of the case which have not appeared in the papers. You were at the opera that night in a box next to the one occupied by the Crane party; you were wearing an emerald necklace which had been purchased that very morning by Mr. Crane; it was with you that Mr. Crane left his house after midnight on that taxi ride from which he never returned. This much we know. What we want of you, Madame Emeraude or Miss Emory, as you prefer, is to fill in the story."

"I see. But why should I satisfy your curiosity and piece out this story for you here and now?"

Jerry suddenly leaned forward and looked into the girl's eyes. "Did you poison my uncle?"

"No," she answered slowly, meeting his gaze. "Did you?"

"No, and there's your reason for telling us your story. You and I are the ones the police suspect of this terrible thing. If neither of us did it, we must stick together and help each other all we can to find out who did it and to clear ourselves, don't you see?"

I noted with surprise and disapproval the tenderness in Jerry's voice. He was evidently falling again under the subtle spell of the frail girl as he had done on the fateful night of the opera. If we yielded to her charm, she would probably twist us both around her slender fingers and transform us from sleuths on the trail of a murderess into knight errants at the service of a fair lady. And yet it was difficult to be stern and cold with her; even I found that I had to keep reminding myself that we were investigating a murder and not simply rescuing a sick girl.

"I know that I should have told what I knew about it long before this," she said. The frightened defiance had faded from her face during Jerry's reassuring speech. "But I somehow wasn't able to 'glue my courage to the sticking point.' It's such a queer story that I couldn't imagine any detectives or policemen believing it, but I would have come forward and told it, really, if I'd thought that what I had to say would be of any help to you, Mr. Paige. I didn't know anything about what had happened until one of our customers left his morning paper on the table after breakfast and I saw the headlines when I was clearing the dishes away. Since then, I've read everything in all the papers."

"You knew then that all the police in the city were hunting for you, didn't you?" I asked sternly.

"Yes, that's what made me so nervous today. I've been spilling things and dropping things all day."

"No one in the restaurant was suspicious of you?"

"No, not at all. All the papers were playing up this mysterious Madame Emeraude as a glamorous and beautiful women. I'm just a poor little waitress that nobody notices much. But I was going to the police if they didn't find out who did it or if I felt my testimony was needed."

"Well, how about the emerald necklace?" I interposed.

The girl looked frightened again. "It hasn't been found yet?" she faltered.

"No," said I. "When last seen it was around your neck."

"I gave it back to Mr. Crane," she said. "He had it with him when we left the Astor Street house last night."

"He didn't have it when he was found dead in the taxi."

"Someone must have robbed him between the time he left me at the hotel and the time that you found him in Oak Park, Mr. McBride."

"Well, suppose you start at the beginning and tell us how you got the emerald in the first place and what happened last night."

CHAPTER 9

"I'VE been a waitress at McGilvary's since last February. It is the first job I've ever held," she began. "I came to Chicago last December with my father. Before that we had been traveling about Europe seeking the best climate for Father. His health broke down after Mother's death three years ago and he gave up his practice in Montreal, Canada, and went abroad taking me as a nurse and companion. We moved about so much for the next two years that I had no opportunity to make any close friends of my own age, but Father and I were very devoted to one another and we were happy together. He was an interesting man and a delightful companion and I was never lonely.

"I hope you aren't bored with all this, but you have to understand my background to understand why I acted as I did with Mr. Crane."

"Tell it your own way," encouraged Jerry. I kept perfectly still.

"Father returned to Chicago to see about some property he had here which was no longer yielding any income. We took rooms at the Congress and he went around interviewing a lot of business men, but I knew very little about our financial affairs and paid little attention. We had spent a lot of money in the preceding years in Europe, but I supposed that we had a safe comfortable income.

"On Christmas Eve Father and I were trimming a little tree in the hotel room. He reached up to put the silver star on the top of the tree and suddenly crumpled to the floor, bringing the tree and all its shiny baubles down on top of him.

"It wasn't until after the funeral that I discovered that Father had left me practically nothing. His investments had not been paying for some time and we had been living on capital. I realized that I was alone in the world and would have to earn my own living some way, but I had no training of any kind.

"McGilvary was the only person I knew in Chicago. He had been our butler back in Montreal when I was a little girl. Father and I had looked him up for old times' sake when we first got to Chicago and had had lunch at the restaurant as his guest one noon. I went to him for help when my money began to dwindle alarmingly and I was really desperate. He offered me a job as waitress. I accepted and have been there ever since. There seemed nothing else for me to do, nowhere else to go. He has been kind to me and patient with me, and I think it gives him a feeling of accomplishment to be in a position to give orders to the daughter of a former employer. I haven't minded the work so much as the loneliness and sordidness of my existence outside working hours.

"Last Saturday morning," the girl went on, "an old gentleman came into the restaurant, sat down at one of my tables and ordered toast and coffee. The place was practically empty as it was only a little after eleven, too late for breakfast and too early for lunch. When I brought his order, I noticed that he was staring at me, not an old man's flirtatious leer but in an absorbed and interested way. I must have shown some embarrassment for he suddenly became aware of what he was doing and apologized for his stare. He ordered another cup of coffee and when I brought it, he kept me at the table and began to ask me questions about myself. I don't usually talk to customers, but there was nothing to call me away. I was feeling lonely and depressed, the old gentleman reminded me somewhat of my father and seemed so kind and friendly that I sat down with him and began telling him all my troubles. He told me that he felt sure that I could find more interesting and congenial work than waiting on tables and offered to help me. He gave me his card and told me to come to see him at his office. His name was Jonathan Crane.

"I was very enthusiastic and grateful at the time, but the more I thought about it, the less reasonable it seemed, and I concluded I'd better stay away from that office. I was still pondering about it, however, when Tuesday morning, (my goodness, was that only yesterday?)

the old gentleman came in again. This time it was nearly twelve and people were beginning to straggle in for lunch. There weren't many at my tables though, and he took the same place as before, ordered one of the luncheon specials and when I brought it, detained me at the table again.

" 'I have something here I'd like to show you,' he said, taking a black velvet case from his pocket. He snapped it open and there lay the loveliest emerald I ever saw, a glowing green jewel on an intricate glittering chain of emeralds and diamonds. Jewels have always fascinated me, although I have never possessed any fine ones and I'm afraid at that moment I forgot where and who I was. I took the case in my hands and stood drinking in the loveliness of its contents, not realizing that I was making myself conspicuous in the restaurant, which was filling rapidly. Mr. Crane took the case out of my hands with a kindly smile, snapped it shut and dropped it into his pocket again.

" 'I just bought it this morning,' he said. 'I had a feeling that you would like it.'

" 'It is the most beautiful thing I ever saw,' I answered.

" 'I had just examined this emerald and made arrangements to buy it when I came in here last Saturday,' he said. 'I stopped in for a cup of coffee to brace me up because of the excitement of seeing the emerald had made me feel wobbly. Stones do affect me. The moment I saw you, you reminded me of that emerald necklace; your fair hair and your green eyes, you seemed the perfect type to wear it. I have been thinking about you and the emerald for two days and that is why I came back today. I wanted to see you together.'

"That seemed a quaint idea, and I went on just to humor him really, 'I'm sure we'd harmonize, that emerald and I; I'd adore to wear it to a ball.'

" 'I don't know about a ball,' said he. 'But do you care for opera?'

" 'Oh, yes,' I answered.

" 'How would you like to wear the emerald necklace to the opera tonight?' he said.

" 'Why, what do you mean?' I gasped.

" 'Don't misunderstand me,' he said. 'I'm not offering to give you my emerald nor even to take you to the opera myself. But I have to go to the opera tonight with my wife and some other people. I don't care much for opera or for my wife's friends but I thought I might enjoy this one if there was a beautiful women in the next box wearing my emerald. I feel that I owe this jewel one evening of splendor before I put it away in a collection to be gloated over by an ugly old man. And you need a night of glamour and admiration too. The adventure would do you both good. How about it?'

"I remember that about then the odor of the boiled cabbage for the business man's plate lunch came drifting through the open kitchen doors. Customers were beginning to crowd in for the noon lunch hour. The place seemed so sordid and smelly and hateful that I felt if I couldn't get away into another atmosphere for at least one evening I would die. A little luxury and excitement seemed most alluring. Of course, I didn't realize how much excitement this innocent sounding little adventure was to bring.

"'I'll do it,' I said quickly. 'I have the afternoon and evening off today. I had rather planned to treat myself to the opera tonight from the gallery.'

"'What time can you get away from the restaurant?' he asked.

"'About two.'

"'Good. I'll meet you on the corner here and we'll make arrangements.'

"Then he left, and the rush of noon customers started. When I got back into the old routine and bustle, the whole thing seemed so fantastic that I really didn't expect to see anyone waiting on the corner at two o'clock. But there he was, a dapper, spidery little figure looking most out of the picture leaning against a corner mailbox on Clark Street.

"'Do you live in the neighborhood?' he asked.

"'Yes, just a few blocks away.'

"We started walking toward La Salle Street and when I pointed out my rooming house to Mr. Crane, he wrinkled up his nose.

"'If we're making this an evening of proper settings,' said Mr. Crane, 'this is hardly the place to start out from. I'll tell you what we'll do, since you have the rest of the day off. Why not come downtown with me? You can get a room at any hotel you like, spend the afternoon getting prettied up, have dinner at your hotel and arrive at the opera in the right mood. Would you like that?'

"The whole thing seemed like a fantastic and glamorous game to me, so I agreed. He waited in the dingy hall of the rooming house while I packed a little bag with the velvet evening gown Father had bought me on our last trip to Paris and my old black party cape which still looked fairly presentable in the evening. Then we taxied to the hotel. I chose the Congress because I had stayed there with my father and it made me feel like those serene days were back again. Mr. Crane gave me a roll of bills and my ticket to the opera. 'Remember,' he said, 'that this is a business proposition. I want you to spend this money on the hotel bills and on getting yourself fixed up, and being frivolous. No hiding it away in the old teapot. Is that clear?' I told him it was.

"He slipped the black velvet case into my hands. 'I'll call for it tomorrow at the restaurant,' he said.

"'And you feel sure that I will be there to give it to you?'

"'I do, my dear, and I also feel sure that you would have difficulty in disposing of it; it's rather unusual and would be easy to trace if stolen.'

"'But suppose I shouldn't want to sell it, but just keep it for myself?'

"'You are unusual yourself,' he answered. 'You'd be almost as difficult to disguise or lose as the jewel.' I've thought of that remark of his often today when I knew that the police were hunting for me. The best way to escape notice in a city is just go about one's usual business. I doubt if any of the people who live in my rooming house or who go to McGilvary's ever bothered to notice that my eyes were green. 'No,' went on Mr. Crane, 'I think I shall find you both at the restaurant tomorrow. Have a good time, remember what I said about the money, and at the opera you will be the mysterious lady with the emerald. I don't believe that we will know each other at the opera. It may save complications.'

"I think it must have been his remark about my being the mysterious lady that made me sign the register at the Congress as Madame Emeraude rather than with my own name. I wanted to forget that I was a waitress in a cheap restaurant and be the grand lady for a night. I spent most of the afternoon in a beauty parlor, indulging in the luxury of a shampoo and a facial once more, and the rest fixing up my velvet dress. By dinner time I really felt that I looked quite presentable. It's quite a responsibility to try to make oneself a fitting background for a jewel like that emerald.

"I dined in state all by myself in the Joseph Urban Room in the hotel, hoping that I looked elegant and sophisticated, but feeling inside like a little girl playing lady. It had been months since I had eaten a meal anywhere but in McGilvary's cluttered, clattery kitchen and you have no idea how wonderful it seemed to sit again at a well appointed table and be served with delicious food by a solicitous French waiter.

"And then the opera. I've gone often to opera in Milan and Paris with Father and I've been yearning to hear the Chicago Civic Opera ever since it opened, but I couldn't afford even the top gallery. I've been starved for good music for a long time and I always did like *Rigoletto*, even if it is considered sentimental and pretty by modern standards.

"I was surprised to find people staring at me. I'm used to going about the city alone and it never entered my head that a solitary woman in a box at the opera would attract any particular attention. It must have been the emerald. It was a bit embarrassing, though I have enough vanity so that I took a certain satisfaction in it. That is, until those notes began to come. Then I got uneasy."

"What notes?" broke in Jerry.

"The first one came at the end of the first act, when I was still lost in the mood of the play. An usher brought me back to reality by pressing something into my hand. He said that a gentleman in the audience had asked him to give it to me. It was a folded piece of paper and on it was penciled in bold, unfamiliar writing: 'Come into the lobby after this act. I must see you.' it was signed, 'Signor Smeraldo.' "

"So, it was to you and not to Uncle Jonathan that Smeraldo sent those notes. That unravels one knot. But how did they happen to be in his pocket when he was found in Oak Park?"

"I gave them to him later that evening. When I went out to Astor Street to—"

"Go on with what happened at the opera," I interpolated. "Jerry, don't interrupt and get her off the track."

"All right. Well, I read the note, but it didn't mean anything to me because I knew no Signor Smeraldo. I thought at first that it must be a message from Mr. Crane and that he had signed it that way as a joke, because *Rigoletto* is an Italian opera and *smeraldo* is the Italian word for his jewel.

"I watched to see if he was going to leave the box, planning to follow him if he did. But he just looked around and gave me a quick, secretive grin and then started talking to Mrs. Crane. He didn't leave his place or give me any sign, so I decided that the note couldn't have been sent by him. I could only suppose then that some masher in the audience was trying to make my acquaintance and I just stayed in my box during the intermission and thought no more about it.

"During the next act, the usher brought another note. It read: 'I mean you no harm. Why do you avoid me? I must speak to you,' again signed Signor Smeraldo. I was a bit bothered and when you and Mr. Crane went out during the intermission, I rose to go too. I met Mr. Crane's eye and must have given him a questioning or appealing look, for he made a gesture to me not to follow him or speak to him, so I stayed where I was, sure then that he had nothing to do with these strange messages.

"At the end of this intermission another folded slip was brought to me. This time it said, 'I will have a car waiting for you at the end of this act. If you come with me, all will be well. This is urgent. Signor Smeraldo.'

"I was beginning to be alarmed, worried mostly about the emerald not about myself, for I knew of course that *smeraldo* is the Italian word for emerald and whoever was writing the notes had his eye on my jewel, although he might have seen the name I used on the hotel register and just used the Italian version of it himself. I thought of stopping Mr. Crane after the performance and making him take his emerald back then. But he seemed so pleased with his little game that I hated to spoil it, and also I was afraid of making trouble for him with his wife. I was sure he had told her nothing about it, and no woman would be pleased to find her husband involved in such an escapade.

"If Signor Smeraldo was only a masher, I felt sure I could cope with the situation. I'd had some practice in that since I'd been in Chicago, so I did nothing and planned to leave a bit before the curtain fell so that I could be sure of getting a taxi and avoiding the crowd. But I was so carried away by the music that the curtain went down before I could collect myself and remember what I had to do. I looked up and saw that your party had already left the box. I hurried out and as I entered the lobby, a dark, good-looking man in evening clothes stepped up to me, bowed formally and said with just a trace of an accent, 'My car is waiting, Madame Émeraude. Permit me at least to take you back to your hotel. It is difficult to find a cab in the after-theatre crush.' He took my arm in a polite but firm grip and started to propel me toward the open door of a waiting limousine. I tried to break away, but he was holding me very tightly and at the same time preserving the deferential attitude of a gentleman escorting a lady to her car.

" 'Let me go,' I said, 'or I will scream and make a scene!' I pulled away from him forcibly enough so that he could no longer disguise his grip upon me as a gallant gesture. When he saw that I would really rather attract unpleasant attention than go with him, he let me go and I hurried down the street in search of a taxi. Everything was taken, and the man soon joined me and walked at my side as if he were helping me find one. I finally hailed an unoccupied cab; the man was still beside me but I thought I could get rid of him. The cabby opened the door. 'To the Congress,' I said, and stepped in. Quick as a flash my pursuer had stepped in after me, managing to follow me in with that same air of being the deferential escort. The taxi started, but I immediately leaned forward and banged as hard as I could on the glass for the man to stop. As I did, I felt a stealthy hand at my throat; the man was after my necklace. I clutched the emerald as tightly as I could through my cloak. The cab stopped and I almost fell out. I felt a backward tug and a wrench as I did so and knew that the chain of my necklace had been torn. But the emerald was still tight in my hand.

"Luckily it was a brightly lit corner; there were a number of people about and a policeman standing near. I hurried towards him. The man, who had started out of the cab after me, drew back in, slammed the door and drove away. The policeman gave me an amused and sympathetic look and hailed another cab for me. I suppose he thought I was just the urban counterpart of the girl who got mud on her shoes, and I didn't enlighten him further.

"I had told the driver that I wanted to go to the Congress, but as we started up the street, I began to collect my thoughts a little. That man was evidently in desperate pursuit, not of me but of my necklace. He knew my hotel. I might very possibly run into the same difficulties in the morning when I started home. I was thoroughly frightened and felt that I should get no sleep until I had returned the emerald safely to its owner. I remembered his home address; I had looked it up that afternoon out of curiosity. So once again I banged on the glass of my cab, changed my directions and settled back, feeling that once I had gotten rid of that glittering green stone, my troubles would be over. I took it out from under my wrap to examine it and discovered that the clasp was broken and a piece of the chain gone entirely, probably left in the lean, wiry fingers of the mysterious Signor Smeraldo.

"I began to get a little nervous as I neared the house on Astor Street, fearing that my visit might make unpleasant complications for Mr. Crane. But it seemed to me the only sensible thing to do. There were still a few lights showing on the first floor of the house. I told my cab to wait and with considerable misgivings went up the steps. To my great relief, Mr. Crane himself answered the door. He seemed surprised to see me, but not in the least angry. He must have noticed my agitation, for he just said. 'Come in, my dear,' and led me into the library. I was still clutching the emerald necklace in my hand and I flung it down on the big, flat-topped desk. He picked it up, looked it over carefully, and then dropped it into the pocket of his dinner jacket.

" 'Sit down and tell me all about it,' he said, pulling up a chair for me before the embers in the fireplace. 'Judging from your appearance and the condition of the chain, the emerald must have brought you more adventure than we bargained for. Permit me to say that you and the emerald sitting there in the next box were also more than I had bargained for. You carried it off very well, my dear, and I hope I haven't got you into trouble.'

"Sitting there in a comfortable chair in the big, dim room, my adventure which had been so terrifying out there in the street, began to seem just a part of the whole fantastic evening, a thrilling adventure instead of an ugly experience. I told him the whole story and showed him the notes which I had kept in my bag. He listened attentively and when I was through, he said nothing except that he thought I had handled the situation very well. We talked a few minutes about the opera and about the possibilities of a better position for me. He offered to ring for sandwiches or something to drink, but I declined; my taxi was waiting and I thought I must get back.

" 'I'm sorry I let my car go,' said Mr. Crane. 'It will be back soon if you care to dismiss your taxi and wait; otherwise I shall see you home myself. I can't have you riding alone and frightened in any more cabs this evening. After thoughtlessly exposing you to one such experience, I must not repeat it.'

"I felt guilty at taking the old man out again so late on such a stormy night, but he insisted. We let ourselves out the front door and went down to the waiting taxi. Mr. Crane still had the emerald necklace in his pocket. The rain which had been falling earlier in the evening had frozen on the streets and now it was snowing and the layer of loose flakes over the ice made driving difficult. Stopping for a red light on Michigan Avenue, our taxi skidded sharply and hit another cab. It merely jolted us but the drivers of both cars got out and began to argue. It had happened only about a block and a half from the hotel, so we decided to walk the remaining distance. Mr. Crane had been rather silent and preoccupied on the drive, and now I noticed that he looked pale and walked a bit unsteadily. I was worried about him and remarked that I ought not to have let him come. He said that he did feel a bit dizzy; he thought perhaps the accident had shaken him more than he realized. He left me at the door of the hotel and went to look for another taxi, and that is the last I saw of him.

"I left the hotel quite early, for I had to be at the restaurant at seven. The lobby was quite deserted when I checked out. I was all through being a grand lady then, and carried my own little bag over to the 'L' station. I had to hurry to get to the restaurant on time and serve stacks of wheats and sunny-side ups until after nine o'clock. It wasn't until then that I happened to glance at the headlines of a paper a late breakfaster had left on his table. When the full significance of what I read dawned upon me, my knees became so weak I had to sit down at the table I was supposed to be clearing in order to collect myself. I've followed everything that has been in the newspapers since and have been in torment.

"That's all I know about the death of Jonathan Crane. I realize it is a queer story that I can hardly expect to be believed."

"I know Uncle Jonathan and that's just the sort of thing he would do," said Jerry thoughtfully. "I believe your story, Miss Emory. The difficulty will be to convince Daggett that you are telling the truth."

"You've given your account of things very clearly, Miss Emory," I added, "but there are a few questions I'd like to ask."

"Very well; I'll answer them if I can."

"The notes which you quoted were found in Mr. Crane's overcoat pocket. Can you account for that?"

"Yes, I gave them to him when we were talking in his library. He said he thought the fellow ought to be tracked down and was going to use the notes as evidence or something."

"You said he put the emerald in the pocket of his dinner jacket. You are sure that he did not remove it before he left the house with you?"

"No, I'm quite positive that it was still there. I really didn't think of it again until we were in the taxi and then I thought it was odd that he hadn't put it somewhere for safety."

"You know, of course, that the emerald was not found upon Mr. Crane. You have no idea where it can be?"

"None whatever. I only know I saw him put it in his pocket. You were the next person to see him after he left me. Perhaps you have it."

I gave the girl a startled glance and Jerry laughed. "That is an excellent theory; no one has thought of that before," grinned Jerry. The girl's attitude toward me had been faintly antagonistic from the first, while the undercurrent of feeling between the girl and Jerry was obvious even under the strained circumstances of the occasion.

"Do you remember," I went on, "seeing a tray containing two glasses on the library table?"

"Yes," answered the girl in a low voice.

"What was in the glasses?"

"One was empty, just some melting ice in the bottom of it. The other one, a little one, had green liquid in it."

"Did Mr. Crane drink this green liquid when you were in the room with him?"

"Yes," answered the girl, and her white face showed that she understood full well what I was driving at. "We were just leaving the room when he said, 'By Jove, I've forgotten to take my medicine in all this excitement,' and he went back and tossed off the potion in the little glass. Oh, if only he hadn't remembered about it, or if I could have stopped him, he'd be alive today, wouldn't he?"

The girl was close to hysterics. Jerry rose from his chair and took her hand. "You couldn't help it," he said soothingly; "you didn't know."

"Where were you sitting while you were talking to Mr. Crane?" I asked.

"In front of the fireplace."

"Then you would both have had your backs to the French windows

67

that opened on the balcony?"

"Yes, I suppose so."

"Do you think that anyone could have opened the French doors and stepped inside the room without your seeing or hearing him?"

"It is possible. The room, I remember, has a soft, deep carpet and we were talking very earnestly."

"Do you know why Mr. Crane went out to Oak Park after he left you?"

"I have no idea. I supposed of course that he would go right home, particularly as he was feeling ill. It seems very strange."

"It doesn't make sense at all," interposed Jerry, "but so much that has happened in the last twenty-four hours doesn't."

"Let's hope Daggett won't feel that way about this story you've just told us, Miss Emory," said I "I'd better see if I can get him on the wire. He's going to be sore as hell that we didn't call him in the first place."

"I don't see why we have to tell him tonight," stalled Jerry. "After all, we discovered Miss Emory for ourselves."

"Where do you get that 'we' stuff? I found her and I'm working with Daggett on this case," said I firmly and went to the telephone.

Daggett was out but had left a number, and after several calls during which Jerry and the green-eyed girl watched me without making a sound, Jerry looking glum and reproachful and the girl looking scared to death, I finally got the superintendent on the wire.

"What! You've got Madame Emeraude?" he bawled when I had given him the news. "Where are you? Where'd you find her? For God's sake, hang on to her until I get there."

"We're at Jerry's apartment," I said. "We'll wait here for you."

"So Daggett is coming over here, is he?" grumbled Jerry.

"Yes, and I think we'd better clear away this dinner debris. And I think, by the way, since I've got to keep on the good side of the old boy, that we'd better not mention that we sat here and ate a square meal and talked it all over before we called him. Come on; let's wrastle these dishes into the sink and clear away."

CHAPTER 10

THE EXCITEMENT of finding the mysterious green-eyed lady lady had entirely driven from my mind the remembrance of my date with Violet. I didn't think of it until after Daggett had arrived and Celia Emory was once more launched into her fantastic tale. She told it more falteringly under Daggett's cold and quizzical stare and somehow it seemed less convincing than when she had recounted the adventure to Jerry and me over the dinner table.

I was acutely uncomfortable, worried about Jerry, embarrassed for the poor little waitress, and nothing new was coming out of the account even under Daggett's expert questioning. Therefore, when my eye caught the little banjo clock on Jerry's wall and I saw that it was almost nine o'clock and I remembered that I had a date with Violet at eight-thirty, I decided to get out of the place.

"Sorry, just remembered I have a date and I'm late for it now," I said and made a dive for my overcoat. Jerry looked as if he thought I was deserting him but I went on down the hall, rang for the elevator, put a call through to Violet from the lobby. She seemed a bit nettled because I was late, but I soothed her down and said that I would pick her up in a taxi in a few minutes.

My taxi was chugging at the appointed corner when Violet came tripping down the block on her spikey French heels.

"Hello," she chirped. "I thought when it got to be eight-thirty and you didn't phone that you'd forgotten all about me."

"I got tied up and couldn't get to a phone," I lied cheerfully.

"Well, it's all right, but I'd have looked pretty silly if you hadn't turned up, because I told Briscombe I was stepping out and he was furious and tried to stop me and we had a fearful row over it. If you'd let me down, I would have looked a fair idiot, wouldn't I?"

"Did you tell him who you were going out with?"

"Yes, I did, and he didn't think much of it." Violet giggled with obvious satisfaction. "He said you were just taking me out to pump me for information about the Cranes, but I told him he was just jealous."

"I'm sure he was, and I confess I'm flattered at the idea. But he'd better not try anything with my girl. This is my night, *n'est ce pas*, baby?"

Violet giggled again. She seemed in a merry mood, delighted to get away from the dreary murder mansion. She thought the joint where I took her was "just darling," flirted shamelessly with the bartender while we leaned at the bar for our first drink, eating potato chips and listening to a piano player rambling along the keys of a baby grand tucked in behind the bar. I dragged her off to a booth for our second and third cocktails and she became suddenly grave.

"Do you think jealousy is a sign of love, Mr. McBride?"

"Gracious, I hope not," said I. "I'd hate to have to be jealous of Briscombe; he's twice my size and hot brown eyes always did make me nervous."

"You're silly," giggled Violet. "You know perfectly well you're only chaffing me. You don't care a fig for me really. You just brought me out to see if you could pump some information out of me for your precious case, now didn't you?"

"I believe in combining business with pleasure whenever possible. It's the ability to find joy and inspiration in my work that has made me the success I am."

My mock gravity sent Violet off into more giggles. "I don't know how much of a success you are, but I think you're cute even if you are a sleuth. And if you can find anything important in my chatter, you'll be the first one that has."

"So it's cute you think I am," I sighed. "Now confess you went out with me just to make Briscombe jealous."

"No, not just for that, but it did set me up a little when I found that he minded. It's hard to tell about Briscombe; sometimes I think he likes me a lot and sometimes he's awfully indifferent. But I don't think he'd be jealous if he didn't care about me, do you?"

"Indeed not," I assured her. "How long have you and Briscombe been going together?"

"Oh, just a little over a month. He's been chauffeur for the Cranes for about two months, but he didn't pay any attention to me at first. I thought he was good-looking but kind of snooty and I was off chauffeurs anyhow. The one before him was a terrible washout and fresh— oh, my!"

"Where did Briscombe come from?"

"He was chauffeur for some friends of Mrs. Crane in the East before she hired him. Came out here with references from them. I don't know why he came to Chicago or what he did before that. He doesn't talk about himself much."

"Did he have any other girl before he started going with you?"

"No, I don't think he did. Of course the missis takes up most of his time, she uses the car a lot. I had another boy friend then myself; he was a nice fellow, worked for Western Union, but he got sent to Cedar Rapids."

"You seem to be a very popular young lady; no wonder Briscombe gets upset over you."

"He hasn't any reason to be, really. I haven't gone out much or cared about anybody since I met him."

"So he hasn't had to be jealous of anybody but me. I'd say you were letting him off pretty easy."

"Well, there was one other time," said Violet, dimpling coyly. "He took me to a dance last Wednesday night, just a week ago, at a ballroom up north. The Cranes were at a dinner party in Wilmette and Briscombe didn't have to call for them until midnight. I knew quite a lot of fellows at this place and I was having such a grand time that I didn't want to leave when Briscombe had to go, and he said I could stay and he'd come back for me later. Just after he left one of the boys introduced me to this Italian fellow; he said that he had asked to meet me."

"I suppose he had hot brown eyes?"

"I'll say he did, and so did that girl Maxine he'd brought. And she didn't like it very well when he danced three dances straight in a row with me and I didn't have any partner to trade off with her. He didn't pay any attention to her. He had a hot line too. He was the most distinguished-looking Italian I ever saw. He was no banana peddler, you could tell that."

"What was his name?"

"As a matter of fact, I never did get it. The orchestra was playing and there was a crowd around when I was introduced to him and I never was good at names, 'specially foreign ones. He told me to call him Ben."

"Oh," I said. "And what did Briscombe have to say when he came back?"

"Plenty. The crowd had thinned out a bit and the orchestra was feeling good-natured and played anything Ben asked them to. We were doing a tango step in the middle of the floor; I didn't know much about the tango, but Ben led me through it so surely that I was stepping out like a regular señorita and we had most of the rest of the crowd backed against the wall looking at us. I saw Briscombe come in and stand watching us stiff as a poker with an unpleasant look in his eyes. We took a few more swoopy glides and then without waiting for the music to stop, Briscombe marched out to the center of the ballroom, grabbed me by the shoulder and swung me around. He said something about having made enough of an exhibition of myself and that we'd have to go home. He hardly spoke to me on the drive back, and when we got to the house, he told me that if I ever went out with that Italian, he'd never have anything to do with me again."

"Nice boy. And how did your friend Ben take this caveman stuff?"

"Oh, he was just rather sneeringly polite, bowed to me and said something about turning me over to my chauffeur. I don't think that went over very big with Briscombe either."

"I should imagine not. Did Briscombe and this Italian know each other?"

"No, I don't think so. I asked Briscombe what he was getting so excited for, I'd danced with plenty of other men. And he said yes, but I'd never put on such a show with any of them. I don't think Ben was acquainted with Briscombe. He knew he was a chauffeur, of course, on account of his uniform."

"Did you and Ben get any talking done or were you too busy making your feet go in those intricate steps?"

"Oh, I always manage to get some conversation in some way," Violet giggled. "You know, Mr. McBride, you're an awfully easy person to be with. I sort of feel that you have my number and like me just the same, so I can just be myself."

"That's fine, little girl, go right ahead. Besides I can't imagine any better pose for you. But go on with your story. It's very interesting. You really ought to write up your adventures and call the novel *The Vicissitudes of Violet*. But to get back, what did you and Ben talk about? Can you remember?"

"Nothing important, let me see. Oh, yes, he asked me quite a lot of questions about the Cranes. Someone had told him I was a maid there. He asked me if I had ever seen Mr. Crane's jewel collection and I told him I had and described some of the pieces for him. He asked if Mrs. Crane wore the jewels and I told him about how Mr. Crane made a collection of them but wouldn't let anyone wear them and Mrs. Crane

71

never had a chance even to look at them unless he got them out for her. He seemed to think that was very odd; in fact he was rather upset about it and asked me a lot of questions about the relations between them and if she went out with other men. He even wanted to know if there was anything between Mrs. Crane and Briscombe. He said he thought it was dangerous for an old man to have such a handsome chauffeur. I thought he was getting pretty nosy and tried to steer the conversation to something else, tried to make him talk about himself— men usually like that—but I couldn't get much out of him."

"Have you heard from him or seen anything of him since?"

"No, and I wouldn't go out with him anyway, because I wouldn't want Briscombe to get really angry. I like to tease him, but I'd be scared as a rabbit if he ever got really sore at me. There's something kinda caveman about him that scares me at times, but I like it really, I guess."

"Who did you think it was on the telephone this afternoon? You said you thought you had recognized the voice."

"You do put two and two together, don't you? Yeah, I thought it was my Italian friend Ben, but it couldn't have been or he would have said something to me."

"Did you give Mrs. Crane the message from the furrier?"

"Yes, I did."

"What did she say about it?"

"She acted kinda funny about it. Asked me several times exactly what the man said and what his voice sounded like and then a little later I heard her sending Briscombe over there with a note. Seems like a lot of fuss over a rip in a coat sleeve, doesn't it?"

"Yes, it does," I agreed.

"I said something like that to Mrs. Crane and she didn't answer, but just froze me up with that icy stare of hers. She can do it, all right. She's been cross as a bear all day."

"She didn't object to your going out tonight?"

"No, I thought she seemed sort of relieved."

"I wouldn't want to get you into any trouble," I said, as I helped her into her coat. "You must watch your step in that house for the next few days and don't forget, if you need any help, don't hesitate to call on me."

"What do you mean?" whispered Violet, fixing wide hazel eyes upon me.

"Just that there has been a murder committed in that house and the murderer is still abroad. Be careful. That's all."

"Oh, dear," whimpered Violet. "I thought I could get away this evening and have a bit of fun and now you're scaring me worse than ever, just when it's time for me to go back to that terrible house."

"I didn't mean to frighten you, but don't talk too much and watch your step!"

Violet was very quiet in the taxi on the way back. "Let me off at the entrance to the alley," she said, as we turned into Astor Street. "My latch key is for the back door and I don't think I'd better be riding up to the front in a taxi tonight."

I dismissed the cab and piloted Violet past back fences and garages to the Cranes' gate.

"Briscombe's in," remarked Violet, looking up at the only square of light which showed on the third floor of the house. "That's his room; the car is in the garage. It's Virtue's regular night off and Mrs. Crane told him to go, though he thought he ought to stay to answer the door and the telephone. Mrs. Bruns is always asleep by this time. Well, good night, I enjoyed the evening and I hope you learned enough to make it worth while for you."

"I'm sure your company is worth any number of cocktails," I said, ignoring the edge of irony in Violet's remark. "I'm sorry not to be in better form myself. Good night and good cheer."

I watched her run lightly up the steps, and even after she had let herself into the house and slammed the door, I stood in the yard puzzling over the events of the evening. Then I turned and walked slowly toward the passageway that led between the houses to Astor Street. But just as I was about to duck into the passageway, I saw that a man was standing at the other end of the passage, his figure silhouetted against the lights from the street. It was dark at my end of the passage and I shrank back unnoticed against the wall. The other man looked up and down the street, then apparently feeling sure that he was unobserved darted into the passageway and swung himself up on the little balcony of the library. Immediately the French doors opened; someone must have been watching inside. The man's figure was illumined for a fleeting instant by the lights from the room, and then he entered the room and the light was blotted out by the hasty closing of the doors. If someone was waiting for the man and had opened the doors for him, he had a legitimate right to be in the house; yet his mode of entry was certainly unusual and this was no time to overlook any strange occurrences. Whereupon I crept silently down the passageway likewise, swung myself up onto the balcony, yet hardly with the ease and swiftness with which the other man had accomplished it. Must be a limber fellow, I thought, as I hauled myself over the iron railing.

The door had been tightly closed and evidently locked as it showed no signs of yielding to my careful pressure. The red velvet curtains were drawn, but one of them was caught back in its lower length and squatting down and gluing an eye to the crack, I was able to see into the room. Mrs. Crane, again swathed in the black Gallenga gown with its gold decorations, was standing facing the door and speaking in a manner which indicated both urgency and distress to her visitor. I could see only a piece of the man's back as he stood apparently quite unmoved by the woman's eloquent and pleading gestures. He was still wearing his black overcoat, his hair was dark and gleaming "patent leather," and he was lacking an inch or two of his companion's height. I strained my ears to try to catch something of their conversation, and in my concentration on the windows failed to hear the stealthy footsteps

73

in the passageway. Suddenly an arm was flung suffocatingly around my neck. I was strong and usually pretty quick, but this time I had been caught off my guard. I struggled madly with this black shape which had caught me unawares, lost my footing, clutched wildly for the iron railing of the balcony but missed it. Then there was a sickening drop, the heavens burst forth into stars and comets for a lurid moment before blackness descended over everything.

CHAPTER 11

I SEEMED to be rising from the murky depths of a deep black pit in which I had been lying for a long, long time. As I rose, my body swayed in the narrow well and my head crashed against rough sides sending shooting pains down my spine.

"Can't you take a little care about my head?" I shouted up to whoever it was who was hauling me up from the pit.

"You ain't been takin' very good care of it yourself, brother," said a thick, unfamiliar voice way up at the top of the pit.

I opened my eyes and found myself staring up into a shadowy unfamiliar face. I was puzzled by the bare brick walls that rose on either side of me. Then my eye caught the black outline of the wrought iron balustrade and I remembered what had happened. This creature bending over me must be the man who had knocked me off the balcony, but I didn't feel up to hitting back at the moment. Instead I muttered, "Who are you?" in a tone which I intended to be ferocious but which came out in kind of a quaver.

"Coming out of it, eh?" said the man. "Well, my name's Murphy and I almost stepped on you when I tried to take a short cut through here over to the alley. You live around here?"

"No," I answered shortly.

"Well, how'd you come to lying in here with your head cut open, son?"

"I was taking a short cut, too, and must have slipped and hit my head against the wall."

"Okay, now I'll tell one. Maybe you did hit the wall, but it looks to me as if somebody had pasted you one. You'd better come along with me and let me fix that pan of yours. I live on this alley."

I was still a bit suspicious, but as I was too weak and bewildered to protest, I let the stranger help me to my feet. I found that I was wobbly and giddy, my head ached with great throbs of pain and my neck was stiff and sore. The Crane house was completely dark, not a crack of light showing anywhere. I looked at my wrist watch and saw by its radium dial that it was just a little past eleven-thirty. It had been after eleven when I left the cafe with Violet so that I couldn't have been unconscious for more than ten or fifteen minutes.

What had happened to Mrs. Crane and her porch-climbing visitor? Who could have attacked me on the balcony? Had my assailant intended to leave me lying in the passageway or had he been frightened away by the approach of this stranger before he could finish the job? Or was this big fellow with the thick voice who seemed so kind and solicitous really the villan in the case?

But as these questions jostled each other confusedly in my aching head, my rescuer, a tall, angular fellow, slid a long arm around me and began half leading, half carrying me toward the alley.

"Did you see anyone come out of that passageway as you came along?" I asked.

"No, I wouldn't a seen you, maybe, if I hadn't tripped on you."

"Were the lights on in the Crane house when you came by?"

"Nope; it was all dark as I remember."

"You didn't see anyone around there at all?"

"There was a man with a black beard standing in front of the house when I came along, but he moved on down the street as I came by. I noticed him 'cause you don't see many of them black spade-shaped beards around here."

Rakowitz wears a black spade-shaped beard but how did he fit into this picture? I thought.

Mr. Murphy had now stopped in front of a little square brick building facing on the alley and was fumbling for his key with one hand while he held me up with the other. He flung the door open upon a neat, cozy, shabby room. A base burner in one corner gave off a glowing warmth very grateful to my chilled stiff body. The fellow insisted on my lying down on the room's one couch which apparently did duty as my host's bed by night and his davenport by day. After he finished bathing and bandaging my wounds, he returned with a pitcher of glowing red wine.

"Wild grape," he said proudly, "made by yours truly out of grapes I picked myself. It's two years old and pretty good.

"Yeh, me and my kid brother go out every fall and load up on wild grapes, there's lots of them around here. The kid has a car. I got a barrel going now in my store room in back there, it's still bubbling a bit."

"Nice little place you have here," I murmured. "Live all by yourself?"

"Yeah, I got a little store over on Clark Street—cigars and magazines and stuff. I used to room up near there but then I heard about this little dump. It used to be a garage, but it wasn't being used for anything so I fixed it up with the owner to come and live here. I like having a little place of my own, and I don't need no woman to take care of it, neither."

"You said it. This has a sea-going look to it."

"Where you live, old-timer?"

"Oak Park."

"Say, you can't go way out there tonight, not in the shape you're in.

You'd better bunk right here with me. You stay on the couch and I'll just park the body in the old Morris chair. The back lets down and it's perfectly good sleeping. I've slep' there before lots of times when my brother was staying in town with me. I c'n sleep most any place."

"Sure thing, but I don't like to take your bed," I protested, not very heartily, however, as the prospect of any kind of exertion was highly distasteful to me just then.

"You needn't think you're going out again alone with that busted head."

I began taking off my shoes.

"You know," said Murphy as we were getting ready to turn in, "I always thought this was an awful respectable neighborhood, but there's been a lot of funny things happening lately. There's all this excitement about old man Crane being poisoned. He lives in this block, you know, and I've had some disturbances myself and have been snooping around a bit. That's how I happened to find you."

"Why? What's happened?"

"Well, when I came home this evening after dinner I found that someone had forced the lock on my door, not such a hard job; it's just an ordinary lock, but there were scratches around and the catch was broken where someone had jimmied it. I knew as soon as I stepped in that someone had been here, because everything was out of line, but not really mussed up; the fellow had evidently taken his time and tried to put things back, knowing I would be gone all day. But I've got everything so methodical around here I can tell when anything's been moved. This guy had pawed through everything, but there was nothing missing. I can't imagine what he coulda been after. There ain't a thing in the place worth breaking in for, unless someone wanted some wine. But there wasn't none of that took, though he'd rummaged around in my cupboard and shifted all the empty bottles and everything."

"That is queer, isn't it?"

"Yeah, and tonight while I was fixing your bandage I'm pretty sure I saw someone trying to look in the window. That's another reason I didn't want to let you out alone tonight."

"You know anybody at the Crane house?"

"Just by sight is all. The high-falutin' chauffeur of theirs drives past here when he puts that swanky foreign car away and he buys tobacco at my shop sometimes."

"Well, let's turn in. I'm dead."

"How about another glass of wine for a nightcap?"

"Suits me."

"Step into the brewery," said Dan, ushering me into the little back closet where an ironbound barrel was reposing in a home-made cradle. He opened a cupboard full of bottles, those on the top shelves filled with glowing red liquid, those on the lower shelves empty. "I'm collecting empties to bottle off this year's brew when it's ready. Takes a lot of bottles for twenty-five gallons of wine. Whenever I see a nice-looking bottle, I lug it home." He took down a full bottle from the top

76

shelf, poured out two glasses. We tossed it down and then sought our respective couches.

I fell immediately into the deep sleep of exhaustion and did not wake until I heard the sound of a key in the lock the next morning. Dan entered all dressed in his outdoor clothes. I sat up with a start.

"Where in hell have you been and why didn't you wake me up before? Good grief, it's after nine o'clock!"

"I went over to open up the store at seven-thirty and then I had to stay until my assistant came. I left him there now and came back to see how you were getting on. Brought you an egg sandwich for breakfast." He dragged a square oil-paper package from his coat pocket.

"The Crane inquest is at ten; I must shove off in a hurry."

"I'll heat up the coffee while you dress," said Dan. "Say, you didn't tell me you had something to do with the Crane case."

"Oh, I'm just covering it for my paper," I said casually.

"Yeah, well here's another item for your paper. My shop was broken into last night. The lock on the back door was forced and everything turned topsy-turvy when I got there this morning."

"Gosh, that's too bad. Did you lose much?"

"No, that's the funny part of it. They took some change that was in the cash register, wasn't more than five dollars, but it looks as if that was done just for effect because everything in the place was sort of pawed over, but nothing missing that I could see. Of course, I just straightened up in a hurry and haven't taken any inventory. Looks like the same kind of a job they did here at the shack except that they were in more of a hurry and didn't put things back. The nightwatchman goes past every half hour."

"You must have something that somebody wants and wants pretty desperately. Haven't you any idea of what it can be?"

"Not the foggiest! I never keep much money around, either here or at the shop. There's nothing much to steal over there except boxes of cigars and a few fountain pens, but there weren't none of them missing."

"What about the raid on this place? Is there something valuable here, something you've acquired recently that some particular person might want?"

Dan shook his head slowly but emphatically, so that his shocky hair fell into his eyes. I gulped down the coffee which was bitter but neither hot nor strong, ate most of the egg sandwich on which the grease was beginning to congeal. I peered up into Dan's mirror to comb my hair and saw the bandage.

"Gee, I can't go out with this gory-looking headpiece," I exclaimed.

"You got an open cut there; you got to have something over it. Sit down and I'll do you a nice neat little plaster."

This took more time in spite of the fact that Dan's big clumsy-looking fingers were surprisingly light and quick with the gauze and plaster. That done, I was just struggling into my overcoat when Dan came grinning in from the back room.

"Here's a little souvenir I fixed up for you," he chuckled, handing

77

me a package wrapped in brown paper.

"Thanks a lot, but what is it?"

"Just a little bottle of my wine. Maybe you'll need a little bracer after the inquest, eh?"

"Fine idea, that's swell of you," I assured him with the private thought that it was going to be a nuisance to lug the bottle with me. However, I couldn't disappoint him so I stuffed it in my overcoat pocket. "And thanks for saving my life and giving me your bed and everything."

"That's all right, old-timer. It was great having you. Drop in any time."

"So long! And if you get any more dope on that robbery, let me know."

"Sure thing," called Dan, as I started down the alley. I didn't take the short cut past the Crane house that morning, for some reason.

CHAPTER 12

THE inquest had begun by the time I arrived and the guard was trying to quiet the people who had been unable to find places in the room and were still milling curiously around the door. I elbowed my way through, showed the guard my press pass and convinced him that I was an important witness, after a bit of argument, and plunged into the crowded room. Jerry was holding a place for me beside him on the witness bench.

"Good heavens!" he exclaimed under his breath when he got a glimpse of my patched head. "That must have been a hot date you had with Violet last night. What were you trying to put over on the little girl when she pasted you that one? I never would have suspected her of packing such a wallop."

"Me and Violet get along just dandy; never a harsh word has passed between us," I muttered back. "I collected this bump later in the evening. Tell you about it afterward. What has happened so far?"

"Nothing much. No witnesses have been called yet."

I had to tell once more how I had found the body of Jonathan Crane in the taxicab, Jerry recited the story of his experience at the opera and his midnight chat with his uncle.

The chemist reported that the autopsy had revealed four grams of strophanthus in the stomach of the deceased, traces of the same poison having been found in the medicine glass from which he had drunk his tonic but not in the tonic bottle, which had not been tampered with, its contents having been analyzed and checked with the original prescription.

Dr. Bentley, Crane's family physician, then testified that he had prescribed the tonic for after-effects of influenza, that Mr. Crane had at various times taken digitalis as a heart stimulant but was not using it at the time he died.

"It would be my opinion," said the doctor in completing his testimony, "that the person who placed this lethal dose in Mr. Crane's glass was familiar with both properties of the drug and Mr. Crane's own physical peculiarities. This dose would not necessarily be fatal in all cases. An overdose of any of the digitalis group of drugs usually causes nausea and vomiting so that the drug is removed from the stomach before it has any fatal effects upon the heart. Any person with a strong heart and a weak stomach would have unquestionably survived such a dose as was given Mr. Crane. Mr. Crane, however, had an unusually strong stomach, he has never even had a twinge of indigestion in the ten years that I have been his physician; but he has a weak heart. Because of the impaired conduction of the heart, the strophanthus caused a ventricular fibrillation, while the nausea, if any, was not severe enough to remove the drug from the stomach."

"Do you think it possible that Mr. Crane took this lethal dose of his own volition?" asked the coroner.

Celia Emory's testimony was the high point of the morning and caused considerable stir among the gentlemen of the press, though the story had broken in the *Leader's* extra the night before, another little scoop for me and George Cobb. The coroner's jury got a flutter from this lily-white maid and her fairy tale too, their eyes gleamed and goggled. It probably was pretty exciting, as inquests go but I was restless and impatient for it to be over.

The coroner finally announced his verdict, that Jonathan Crane had died from the effects of a lethal dose of extract of strophanthus placed in his medicine glass by person or persons unknown.

During the inquest I had scrawled a note and sent it over to Daggett telling him that I wanted to see him after the inquest as I had some news for him. He came edging over immediately after the coroner's verdict was announced.

"Huh, what have you been getting into, young fella?" he said eyeing my broken head.

I told him as briefly as I could the events of the previous evening. "I feel fairly certain that the man was Pirani," I concluded, "and Dan Murphy told me that he saw a fellow with a black beard loitering in front of the Crane house just before he turned into the passageway and tripped over my senseless form, as it were. That sounds like Rakowitz; he's the only black-bearded guy who has crossed our path so far, and we know that Pirani and Rakowitz are in cahoots somewhere along the line."

"Come on," said Daggett shortly. "No use speculating about this. We're going out to see what Mrs. Crane has to say about it."

Virtue answered the door at the house on Astor Street and said that Mrs. Crane had left orders that she would see no one, but that he would tell her that we were there.

I was prowling about among Jonathan Crane's books, when Agatha Crane flowed into the room looking handsome and elegant in modish black crepe. I quickly flapped the book in my hand shut and quietly sat on it during the rest of the interview.

"Really, Inspector," began Mrs. Crane, "I should think that on the day that my husband was to be buried, you could allow me a little peace and quiet. If you have further questions, I should think that it would be only decent and humane to wait until after the funeral this afternoon. Did something important develop at the inquest?"

"Nothing that you don't already know," replied Daggett, "but there is a little matter I want to ask you about. Jim McBride went out with your maid Violet last night."

"I know he did," snapped Mrs. Crane, "and I consider it very bad taste on his part."

"After he left Violet at the back gate," Daggett went on, ignoring this thrust at me, "he saw a man come down the passageway between the houses and climb up to the balcony outside the window there. The doors were opened to him from the inside, McBride says, and the man stepped into the room. Who was that man, Mrs. Crane?"

Mrs. Crane's pose of frosty dignity now shifted to an air of guarded watchfulness. She looked appraisingly from Daggett to me and back again, trying apparently to decide how much was bluff and how much we really knew. I tried to look mild and innocent, thinking Daggett, in spite of the unusual politeness with which Agatha Crane seemed to inspire him, was being forceful enough for both of us.

"Yes, Ben Pirani did call upon me last night," the words came in a low dramatic tone after a portentous pause. "He sent word that he was coming and I met him in the library."

"Why haven't you told us this before? You knew we were hunting for this man."

"I did not know myself until last night. I had heard, of course, that my husband had purchased the emerald necklace from an Italian of that name, but I had no idea that Ben was in America and the name meant nothing to me. He took the name Pirani just for this American trip. His real name is Benedetto Montebruzzi, the same as that of my first husband. He is a cousin of Juliano."

"What did he wish to see you about?"

"He was worried about the necklace. You see, there is a crazy superstition in the family that the necklace must stay in the possession of the Montebruzzis or it will bring bad luck to them all, particularly to the one who has permitted it to fall into alien hands. It is nonsense, of course, but Ben was brought up by his widowed mother and an old great-aunt and he was steeped in superstition as a child. Those things are hard to eradicate once they are fully absorbed. Ben would never have sold it if he hadn't needed money quite desperately."

"Did he think you had the necklace?"

"No, but he thought I might know where it was. You see, Ben

thought when he sold the necklace to Mr. Crane that he was buying it for me and in that way it would be staying in the family and so avert the ill omen. He was very much upset to find that I had never received it."

"Does he still consider you a member of the family?"

"Well, yes, they feel that once a Montebruzzi, always a Montebruzzi." She spoke lightly, but I noticed that she had colored uncomfortably at this seemingly innocent query of Daggett's.

"I told him of course that I had never even seen the necklace except once years ago in Italy when it was in the possession of my husband's elder brother's wife. Ben acquired it when he died a year ago."

"Would it have been inherited by your husband if he had lived?"

"Yes," answered the former Contessa Montebruzzi indifferently. "I suppose it would."

"Had Pirani communicated with you before last night?"

"No."

"Why did he enter by way of the balcony instead of the door?"

"It was entirely his own idea. He was afraid the house might be watched and he didn't want to be seen and dragged into the affair. He wants to go back to Italy as soon as possible and was afraid that you would make him stay here for a trial."

"A man climbed up to that balcony on the night that you husband died. Was that Pirani?"

"I don't know. He didn't mention anything of the sort."

"Where is Pirani living?"

"I don't know. He avoided telling me purposely, because he doesn't wish to be traced, and figured that if I knew his whereabouts I would feel obliged to disclose them to the police if I were questioned, and of course, I would."

"McBride was attacked on the balcony last night."

"I've been wondering how you hurt your head," murmured Mrs. Crane, turning to me with a sympathetic gesture which was belied by the gleam in her sapphire eyes. I suspect that she was pleased that I got knocked off the balcony, served me right for spying on her, no doubt. "I'm sorry you met with an accident, but I can't imagine how it could have occurred. It doesn't seem like Ben to do such a thing."

"Ben was inside the room talking to you," I interposed. "You sure he didn't bring a friend?"

"He was alone, so far as I know. Are you sure you were attacked? Snoopers have been known to lose their balance and fall off balconies, you know."

"Oh, I lost my balance, all right," I admitted calmly, "but only after I had been slugged in the back of the head with a blackjack or something."

"Most unfortunate. But it must have been done quietly and skillfully. It is odd that we heard no disturbance in the library."

"Very odd," I muttered. "By the way, do you know Rakowitz, the furrier?"

"Why, I sent him some work recently," said Mrs. Crane after a pause. "I don't know him personally."

"Did you see him last night?"

"Why, no, naturally not."

"If you hear from Pirani-Montebruzzi again, I hope you will let me know immediately and get his address," interrupted Daggett. "We won't keep you any longer."

"Well, and what do you make of that?" I asked, as we started down the steps.

"She's a clever woman, if not a truthful one," muttered Daggett.

"I bet she knew more than she let on about my busted head too. I'm not such a heavyweight, but I should think if I fell off a balcony with a thud that someone on the other side of the window might notice it. She had her answers pretty well doped out, but she was a bit put out by that question about Rakowitz, did you notice?"

"Yeah."

"I want to hear what Benedetto has to say about this and I have a good hunch where to locate him."

"Rakowitz?"

"Yeah, he's in this somehow and he and Pirani are friends. He helped talk old Schultz into selling the emerald to Crane. On Tuesday morning Mrs. Crane took her fur coat to Rakowitz' furrier shop, drove over with it herself, though she bought the coat at Field's and would normally have taken it back there for repairs."

"Well, let's go. Do you know the address?"

"Yes, it's over in the Wilson Avenue district."

Daggett had a roadster this time so we didn't have to wait for a taxi but piled in and started north. I tried to pump him about Jerry on the way out, but he didn't want to talk to me about Jerry and was noncommittal. I realized from his evasive answers that Jerry was not sitting pretty with the police department, by a long shot.

We soon pulled into the side street just off Wilson where Rakowitz' furrier shop was located. As usual, there was no place to park.

"Hold it," I called, "there's a car moving out just ahead. You can get in there." I hung out the window to get a better view of the other car's movements and saw that it was a blue Isotta Fraschini and the trim figure in the olive-green uniform expertly swinging the wheel to get out of the narrow parking space was Briscombe. He was too intent on his maneuvers to see us.

"Briscombe in the Crane car," exclaimed Daggett as I pointed excitedly. "So he got here before we did. I wonder why."

"Maybe Agatha sent him to try on the fur coat for her," I suggested.

The blue car cleared itself and sped away and Daggett maneuvered into the empty space. The anteroom of the fur shop as we entered smelled musty and furry. A girl with a mop of black hair, cut short and curling away from her vivid face like hyacinth petals, sat at a table reading a novel. She gazed at us somberly with dark gleaming eyes as we entered and murmured a sulky, "Good morning."

"I have an appointment to meet Ben Pirani here," announced Daggett in a premptory tone. "Has he come in yet?"

"He never went out, that I know of," the girl answered with the same sullen air.

"Will you tell him we're here?"

"I just wait on customers. I don't run errands for Pirani," she answered.

"Come on, be a good girl, Maxine," I added, just on chance that this was Maxine, the girl who had accompanied Pirani to the dance the night he had deserted her for Violet and the tango. It was a good shot, for she turned a startled gaze at me.

"I don't know you and I bet Ben doesn't either," she flung at me and bolted into the back room. Daggett and I followed close on her heels. Rakowitz was standing over a cutting table littered with pelts, a big pair of shears in his hand.

"*Ach, du dummkopf!*" he muttered at his daughter. Then he turned to us and said in a deep guttural voice, "I am Rakowitz. What do you want here?"

"We came to see Ben Pirani."

"I know nothing about him. I haven't—"

"Don't waste your time, Rakowitz," interrupted Daggett. "Your daughter has already spilled the beans; we know he's here. Tell him to come out or we'll search the house. You know he is wanted by the police."

"It seems to me that you are making a very big fuss over nothing," interposed a casual, melodious voice with a slight foreign accent, and a young man stepped out from behind a rack of fur coats at the back of the room. He was slender and graceful with shining dark hair and big dark eyes. He answered perfectly to Celia Emory's description of Signor Smeraldo and Violet's account of the "tangoing Italian" at the north side ballroom.

"You are Benedetto Pirani, who formerly lived at —— La Salle Street and who commissioned August Schultz to sell an emerald necklace to Jonathan Crane?" interrogated Daggett.

"That is correct," murmured Pirani.

"Is Pirani your real name?"

"No, my family name is Montebruzzi."

"Why did you change it on coming to America?"

"Because it is an old and famous name, and since I could not live here in the way that a Montebruzzi is accustomed to living, I preferred to keep my identity a secret. I presume you are unable to understand this kind of pride."

"Oh, I can understand it," replied Daggett mildly, "but, of course, the Daggetts have always let the same name do them for all their ups and downs. You haven't used any other names since you came to Chicago, have you?"

"No."

"What was the Crane car doing out in front here a few minutes ago?"

Pirani laughed suddenly, a musical, gleeful but somehow unpleasant laugh. "Oh, that," he chuckled. "Agatha wants her fur coat for the funeral and perhaps she thought I ought to know that you have already discovered that I called upon her last night, via the window."

"Why did you visit Mrs. Crane last night?" Daggett asked.

"Why not? She's my cousin and she had survived a loss. It was only proper that I should call on her. That I came through the window was your fault. If you hadn't set your hounds on my trail, I could have come through the front door like a gentleman. I told her I didn't want to be noticed and she told me that I could come in through the library windows."

"Have you ever entered the house that way before?"

"I'd never entered it at all before."

"Where is the Crane emerald?"

"How should I know? I sold it."

"Did Mrs. Crane's being a cousin by a former marriage have anything to do with your selecting Crane as your purchaser?"

Pirani's dark brows lifted in an amused and quizzical expression. "Perhaps."

"Why?"

"It is more pleasant to deal with friends than strangers."

"How about this superstition that the emerald brings bad luck if it goes out of the family?"

"There is such a superstition, yes."

"Do you consider Mrs. Crane still a member of your family?"

"Did she say I did?"

"She said that in that family it was, once a Montebruzzi, always a Montebruzzi."

That look of sly amusement passed again across his dark, pretty face. "That's right; you can't get away from us," he gurgled.

Daggett didn't seem to care for the way things were going nor for the sullen stares of the black-bearded Rakowitz and his spectacular daughter.

"Get your coat, Pirani," he commanded shortly. "I'm taking you back to headquarters."

"Very well," sighed Pirani with a shrug. "But I must get away in time to attend poor Cousin Jonathan's funeral."

We piled back into the roadster with Daggett driving, Pirani in the middle and me on the outside and headed for the Loop.

"Are you acquainted with Miss Celia Emory?" asked Daggett after weaving through the traffic in silence for several blocks.

"No," answered Pirani shortly. "I know very few young ladies in Chicago."

"H'm," said I, "and I hear you are such a good tango dancer, too. Was that Maxine Rakowitz you were with the night you met Violet?"

"Possibly," answered the Italian scornfully. "Is that why you are dragging me off in this so inconvenient way? To ask me about my engagements with ladies?"

"Partly," growled Daggett. "Jim, do you know where Emory was going after she left the inquest?"

"I have a hunch," I answered. "She and Jerry wanted to talk things over. I think they may be lunching together in his apartment."

"I'll let you off on Surf Street and you round her up and bring her down to headquarters. If she isn't there, find her."

I was thus let off in front of Jerry's apartment building. My surmise was correct; the two of them were there talking over the remains of a lunch and a pot of tea.

"We've got Pirani," I said, breaking into this intimate little scene without ceremony. "Daggett wants you to come down and see if he's the gent that followed you out of the opera, Miss Emory."

"Right away?" asked Jerry.

"Pronto," I replied.

"Okay, we'll be right with you." And Jerry began dragging his and his visitor's coats from the closet. Celia hadn't said anything.

"He didn't say anything about your coming too," I ventured, but Jerry paid no attention to me and I wasn't going to tell him he couldn't come, so the three of us went down and piled into a cab.

Pirani had lost his scornful composure when I saw him again in Daggett's office. He had had his fingerprints taken and his shoe measured to see if it corresponded to the footprints on the balcony, which it did, and he was seething with indignation at such treatment for a member of the noble house of Montebruzzi. He didn't look any too pleased to see Celia either.

"This is Mr. Pirani-Montebruzzi, Miss Emory," said Daggett. "Have you ever seen him before?"

"Yes," whispered Celia. "I saw him Tuesday night at the opera."

"Were you at the opera on Tuesday night, Mr. Pirani?" queried Daggett.

"Yes," replied Pirani smoothly, but his dark eyes were fixed on Celia with a menacing look.

"In your desire to keep your family name unsullied, did you ever call yourself Signor Smeraldo?"

"That was just a little joke between Miss Emory and myself."

Celia gasped and gave him a startled look but said nothing.

"I thought you said you didn't know Miss Emory."

"I know her all right," said Pirani in an insinuating tone, "but I never was sure what her last name was."

"Did you send notes to Miss Emory at the opera asking her to meet you after the performance?"

"Yes. I just happened to be there that evening, saw her in the box alone and thought she might like to have an escort home. I was also curious about the necklace. I recognized it, naturally."

"Where did you know Miss Emory?"

"Oh, I used to flirt with her some at McGilvary's and I've taken her

85

out once or twice."

Celia stared at the man with wide, incredulous eyes and Jerry was obviously controlling himself with difficulty.

"Is this true, Miss Emory?" asked Daggett.

"No," gasped Celia. "I don't remember him in the restaurant and I've never gone out with him. I never saw him until that night at the opera."

"Oh, well," said Pirani with an airy gesture of his long supple hands, "if anything I say conflicts with the lady's story, just omit it. I have no wish to be ungallant, but I couldn't know what her story was going to be. You asked me first. It really doesn't matter."

"Well, let's have your account of last Tuesday's evening," snapped Daggett.

"Nothing much to tell," said Pirani. "I went to the opera alone and was much surprised when I saw Celia in the box wearing my emerald. I had seen her talking to Crane in McGilvary's, but I had no thought that things had gone so far between them. If I had known that Crane was buying the necklace for his sweetie, I would never have sold it to him. I sent Celia those notes signed Signor Smeraldo just as a joke. She knew who they were from right enough. I met her in the lobby after the last act, but she said she had a date with Crane and refused to come with me, so I went home. That is all."

"Miss Emory says that you forced her into a taxi with you."

"Does she indeed?" shrugged Pirani. "Mind if I smoke?" and he drew out a silver case.

"She also says that you tried to take the necklace from her," Daggett went on.

"Now that is going a bit too far," cried Pirani, his dark eyes flashing. "She is trying to cover up the fact that she still has it herself. Crane is dead and dead men tell no tales. She's safe enough."

"You followed her to the Crane house."

"I did nothing of the kind. I tell you I went back to Rakowitz' place. He can tell you. He was still up when I came in."

"You are sure," said Daggett, turning again to Celia who was looking white and stricken, "that this man tried to take the necklace from you in the cab after the opera."

"Yes!" There was a trace of a sob in the monosyllable that made Jerry clench his fists.

"Neither one of us can prove anything," said Pirani lightly. "You'll just have to decide among yourselves whether you will take the word of Benedetto Montebruzzi or of an unknown little hussy of a waitress."

"You damned cad!" cried Jerry, unable to contain himself any longer. He would have hauled off and banged Pirani in the nose right then and there if I had not grabbed him.

"You'd better keep out of this, Paige," growled Daggett. "I didn't send for you anyway. As for you, Pirani, you can go along for the present. But understand that you are not to leave town and notify the police if you make any change of address. You will go on staying with

Rakowitz, I suppose."

"I might as well," muttered Pirani. "I was staying there just because it was cheap and I had no ready money except those damned thousand-dollar bills that the police were watching for. At any rate I can use those without getting policemen on my neck, can't I?"

"Go ahead. Spend all you like, and good-by."

CHAPTER 13

JONATHAN CRANE'S funeral took place at two o'clock on Thursday afternoon. There was a formal service at St. Chrysostom's but I did not wish to be among the gaping crowd which always attempts to follow the coffin of a gentleman whose death has made the newspaper headlines. The service at the grave was private, so I spent the afternoon upon concerns of my own, got the column out and a little after four put through a call to Jerry's apartment just on a chance. Somewhat to my surprise Jerry's voice answered.

"Hello! It's Jim," I said. "You're back early."

"Yes," answered Jerry. "I came right on home from the cemetery and didn't go back to the Crane house. I didn't feel that I'd even be welcome, let alone a comfort to my aunt. I've been sitting here alone, getting more and more jittery. Can't you come over? I need someone to talk to. Got some news that may interest you, too."

"I'll be right over, old-timer."

I taxied over to Surf Street and went right up to Jerry's apartment where I found him slumped in an armchair, morosely sipping at a tall highball glass. He seemed pleased and relieved at my coming and brightened up considerably as he mixed another drink for me.

"Well," he sighed, as we settled down with our whiskey and sodas, "Uncle Jonathan is gone and safely out of trouble, but he certainly left plenty of it behind him."

"Tell me about the funeral."

"It was ghastly. Funerals are a barbaric institution anyway. I know that Uncle Jonathan would rather have been stowed away quietly without any fuss but Aunt Agatha insisted on all the trimmings, music, mountains of flowers, candles and robes. She had herself got up very elegant and picturesque in flowing black chiffons. I met her at the house and escorted her to the church and though she came in on my arm she wouldn't speak to me at all. She kept Violet sitting beside her with the smelling salts all the time we were at the house. And when we got to the church who do you think came sliding into the family pew looking solemn and sympathetic like the perfect sorrowing relative?"

"Benedetto."

"Right, the first guess."

"He is a nervy little squirt. He didn't climb through the stained glass window, did he?"

"I don't know how he managed it but there he was and what is more he went out to the cemetery with us afterward, took Aunt Agatha's other arm in a most tender and solicitous fashion and came right along."

"How did the widow like that?"

"She didn't like it at all, that was obvious. But she couldn't shake him off without appearing undignified before all those people, and that is something Aunt Agatha could never do."

"Why didn't you do something about it?"

"I would have, if Aunt Agatha had given me any sort of a lead. Besides, I was feeling just about as unwelcome myself. It was kind of tough on the old girl to be supported on either side in her hour of sorrow by young men whom she dislikes and distrusts. I couldn't help but be sorry for her in spite of the way she was treating me. If she really believes that I poisoned Uncle Jonathan, she is quite justified, of course, but I wonder if she does. I think she knows a damn sight more about the whole business than I do."

"Well, how about Pirani? Did he go back to the house with her?"

"No, he got into the car all right. When we left the grave, he helped her over the muddy spots and climbed right in after her. There was nothing for me to do but get in too, though I'd rather have walked home. I decided that I wasn't going back to the house for the reading of the will. I had found out beforehand what was in it. Miss Cotton broke down and told me, and I confess I didn't like the prospect of being in the same room with Aunt Agatha when the lawyer explained it to her. I think Pirani would have gone in, if she hadn't said good-by to him very pointedly at the door and given Briscombe instructions to drive him and me wherever we wished to go. I don't think that Pirani would care to tackle Briscombe, so he stayed put. I had a feeling that Briscombe would have enjoyed dumping him back into the car by the scruff of his neck if he had tried to follow Aunt Agatha again.

"Anyway, Pirani and I were left alone in the back of the car. After Aunt Agatha went home, he said he wanted to go back to Rakowitz' so we went on north and Briscombe dropped me off here first. Just before we got to Surf Street, Pirani said that he'd like to have a talk with me sometime very soon. I told him to come on up then and he said that he couldn't come now but that he'd like to come back this evening and made an appointment with me for ten o'clock here at the apartment. Now what do you make of that?"

"Sounds like a lively interview. I'd like to be in on it."

"He said particularly that he wanted to see me alone. But why don't you drop around sort of accidentally about 10:30? In fact you might as well bunk with me tonight. You don't want to go way out to Oak Park and I'd rather not be alone."

"Okay, that's not a bad idea. I'll show up with my nightie about 10:30."

"Now that's settled, what do you say to another highball? Goodness knows, I need one."

"I wouldn't say no. Oh, by the way, I have a bottle of wine in my coat pocket. That marine I stayed with last night presented it to me this morning. It is his own vintage and he's very proud of it, so I couldn't refuse and I've been lugging it around all day. It's not bad stuff. Wouldn't you care to sample it?"

"No, thanks. Whiskey is what I need."

"I'll take it out of my coat pocket while I have it on my mind and leave it here."

I fumbled in my overcoat pocket for the brown paper parcel, pulled it out and stowed it away on a shelf in Jerry's kitchenette. I was later to regret deeply that Jerry's preference for strong liquor had prevented me from opening the wine bottle that afternoon, but the big glasses of whiskey and soda hit the spot at the moment and the wine bottle waited, a silent witness, with its secret still muffled in brown paper.

Between drinks we discussed the various angles of the case, with Jerry getting gloomier and gloomier. Finally I jumped up.

"I've got to push along. I want to have a talk with Tiedemann and do a few other little odd jobs. I'll be back about 10:30, and mind you keep your shirt on with Pirani. You'll glean more that way and what we need is information about that guy."

CHAPTER 14

PROMPTLY at ten-thirty I reappeared at the apartment house on Surf Street. The lobby was deserted except for the night clerk who had dragged an armchair over to the switchboard and was peacefully reading a novel. He looked up inquiringly as I entered.

"I'm going up to Mr. Paige's apartment," I said. "You don't need to ring him; he's expecting me."

"Okay," responded the clerk, returning to his book.

I walked over to the automatic elevator and pushed the button. Nothing happened. I pushed again. These pesky things are always slow, but there was no movement at all.

"Isn't the elevator running?" I asked the clerk.

"What's the matter? Is that thing still on the blink?" growled the man, throwing down his book. "The Redfields just went out and complained that they had to walk down because they couldn't get the elevator, but I thought maybe they were in a hurry and just didn't wait for it. I don't think it's really out of commission because it was working all right about fifteen minutes ago. Some dumbbell has probably left one of the doors open and you know the thing won't go unless both the inner and outer doors are closed tight."

He came over, tried the button himself and as he got no response, heaved a sigh and said, "Well, I guess I'll have to take you up in the freight elevator."

"I could walk," I suggested without enthusiasm.

"Oh, no. It's a long climb up to the ninth and besides, I have a hunch that the thing may be stuck on the ninth floor anyway. The last person to use the elevator was a young fellow calling on Mr. Paige. He must have gone up to the ninth and the car hasn't moved since. I'd have gone to investigate sooner only I was alone at the switchboard and couldn't get away."

During this conversation the clerk had led me down the hall to the other elevator, a big crude affair in which we were soon lumbering upwards.

"How long ago did this other man go up to Mr. Paige's apartment?"

"Oh, about fifteen minutes ago."

"And he hasn't come down?"

"No."

"What did the man look like?"

"He was a dark, foreign-looking young fellow."

That must be Pirani, all right, I thought to myself, and hoped that I wouldn't upset the applecart by breaking in this way. The car stopped at the ninth floor and we stepped out. The clerk walked down the hall with me to the doors of the automatic passenger elevator and peered through the little square window high in the door, but the opening showed only the bare brick wall of the opposite side of the shaft.

"The beastly thing isn't stuck on this floor after all," he muttered. "I'll have to take time out to scout around until I catch it, and just let them keep ringing until I can get back to the board."

"Thanks for bringing me up," I called and went on down the hall to Jerry's apartment while the clerk went slamming back into the freight elevator and creaked away on his search. I listened for a moment at Jerry's door but heard no sound of voices. I gave a mild and tentative rap and the door flew open immediately. Jerry stood there looking very tense and nervous, but there was no sign of his visitor as I looked around his living room.

"Hello," I said cheerfully. "Just thought I'd drop in for a bit of a chat." This was for Pirani's benefit if he should be about.

"Pirani never showed up," said Jerry abruptly. "Come on in."

"That's damned odd. The night clerk just told me that a dark, foreign-looking man had gone up to your apartment about fifteen minutes ago."

"I've been sitting right here since nine o'clock. I don't understand it. You sure that Jordan said the man was coming to see me?"

"Yes, and furthermore the elevator hasn't worked since. Maybe Pirani isn't accustomed to the habits of American elevators and is stuck in it somewhere. Better call the clerk and get this straight. I just took it for granted that your caller was Pirani and that he'd still be here since he hadn't gone through the lobby again."

Jerry went to the phone. "There's nobody at the switchboard," he growled.

"The chap must be still out looking for the elevator," I suggested. "Keep on trying. He'll be back in a minute 'cause he had the board on his mind all right."

Jerry stayed at the phone and presently a breathless voice answered from downstairs.

"This is Mr. Paige, Jordan. Was there a man calling for me about fifteen minutes ago? . . . He came up in the elevator and hasn't gone out again? . . . Oh, yes, Mr. McBride is here, but I haven't seen the other man and I was expecting him. By the way, did you find the elevator? . . . You didn't. Well, you stay at the desk and keep an eye out for that dark visitor of mine; I don't want to miss him. Mr. McBride and I will go and look for the elevator."

"So," said I, as Jerry hung up, "you are letting me in on a big game expedition, hunting elevators."

"Yeah," returned Jerry absently. "There is something funny about this. Jordan said he looked on every floor and couldn't find the car and Pirani was the last person to ride in it headed for the ninth floor. He couldn't have gone out again unless he walked down while Jordan was riding the freight or climbed down the fire escape. We might as well go find the elevator. I'm getting the jitters sitting here, waiting."

"Okay. I'll get my trusty elevator gun and accompany you," I snatched up a malacca walking stick of Jerry's and started down the hall with what was meant to be the stealthy tread of an African elephant hunter, but Jerry was not in a mood for clowning. He stopped in front of the elevator and peered into the empty shaft. He tried the door, which slid back easily under his hand.

"That's funny," he cried. "The doors usually won't open unless the car is on the floor. Holy cats, give a look! There she is, stuck halfway."

Now that the doors were open we could look down the shaft instead of merely straight across it from the little window, and there was the black top of the elevator just about at the level of the floor.

I peered down at the top of the motionless car and then chanced to glance up at the ignition box at the upper corner of the door frame. A tiny scrap of white protruding from the black box caught my eye. I reached up and pulled out a folded bit of white paper which had been wedged into the apparatus.

"Some one must have stuffed that in to break the contact," exclaimed Jerry. "Shut the door and push the button and see if the car will come up now."

I did so but instead of responding to our summons, the car sank from sight and we saw only the steel ropes sliding past the window.

"Oh, I forgot," grinned Jerry, "It's an intelligent elevator with a good memory. It keeps on going where it was told to go before the contact was broken."

The ropes ceased to slide and then started moving in the other direction. "She's coming up," announced Jerry.

Just then we heard a wild shriek muffled but terror-stricken, succeeded by another and then another, growing louder and more blood curdling. It was the piercing shriek of a woman in the extremity of fear. Jerry and I could only look at each other in wild apprehension. Then came another soul-tearing howl and the light of the elevator appeared in the square piece of glass in the door. The gates were flung back with a crash and a girl, her blue eyes glazed with horror in a livid white face, stumbled out of the car and flung herself, sobbing hysterically into Jerry's arms.

Propped in the far corner of the car was the cause of her terror—a crumpled, blood-soaked figure. He was sitting in a sprawled position on the floor of the car, his back leaning against the corner walls, his black overcoat open and crumpled under him, his head lolled to one side with dark eyes open and horribly staring. His black fedora hat lay beside him in a pool of blood, the patent leather hair hung in tousled black strands across his dank forehead. He was an object to send any young lady into justifiable hysterics. I thought immediately of another sprawled and lifeless figure in a black overcoat. What evil force had taken the lives of these two, for the deaths must be linked in some mysterious way?

"My God, it's Pirani!" groaned Jerry, as he stared across the golden head of his sobbing burden at the slumped ghastly figure in the elevator.

People were now running from every door along the corridor. Jordan, the night clerk, and the manager of the hotel emerged from the creaking freight elevator demanding to know what all the shouting was about.

"There is a dead man in the elevator," I said briefly. "Jordan, notify Inspector Daggett at police headquarters immediately and you'd better call a doctor too, although I'm quite sure it is too late for him to be of any use."

"Gosh!" gasped Jordan after a glance into the car. "No wonder Miss Burke let out a yell. I would myself. And say, it's that fellow that was asking for Mr. Paige, the one I told you about."

"I know it is," I snapped. "You go make that call."

Tyson, the manager of the apartment, shot a swift, suspicious look at Jerry. "Do you know this man, Mr. Paige?"

"Yes," replied Jerry in a husky whisper and shifting Miss Burke over to cry on his left shoulder. "He calls himself Benedetto Pirani. I had an appointment with him here at ten o'clock but he didn't come—that is, I didn't see him."

A doctor and two policemen suddenly appeared from somewhere. The doctor made a nervous and gingerly examination. "The man is dead, but he was killed not more than half an hour ago, I should say. The body is still warm. He was stabbed through the heart with a black-handled knife which is still in the wound," reported the medico, rising from the horrid bundle on the elevator floor.

Just then there was a clatter on the stairs and a little brunette, with red satin mules clacking on her bare feet and a gaudy coolie coat flung over her black satin pajamas, came rushing up to Jerry's weeping protégée, who continued to cling to him like a vine to a church tower. "Val, you poor darling, whatever has happened?" she cried.

"Oh, oh, Betty, it is just too awful!" Valerie Burke relaxed her convulsive hold on Jerry and transferred herself to the arms of her friend. "I'd just come back from the theater and had rung for the elevator. Jordan said it wasn't working and that he'd take me up in the freight, and then I said it must have got fixed because I could see the ropes moving. It stopped on the ground floor and I got in. The lights were turned off, which was funny because they are always on, but I could see well enough to find the buttons in the light from the lobby. I got in and turned on the top light and pushed the button for our floor and then I looked around and there was this— Oh, I shall have nightmares about it the rest of my life. I was all shut in with it, the car was moving and the doors were shut and I was too scared to move, just shut up in a moving elevator all alone with that awful thing!" And Valerie began weeping afresh all over the gaudy coolie coat this time.

"You'd better take her up to the apartment and put her to bed, Miss Bennett," said Tyson. "She's had a bad shock."

Betty Bennett lead her tear-stained friend away, up the stairs to their apartment. One of the cops began shooing away the curious crowd which had now swelled to considerable proportions and the other began asking Jerry and me questions. Into this scene burst Daggett, looking pretty grim. He took a quick look at the body, shot a keen glance at Jerry.

"Well, McBride, you seem to be Johnny-at-the-rathole when anything happens, don't you? What were you doing here?"

"I came over to spend the night with Jerry," I answered. "Got here at ten-thirty. Jerry and I found the body."

"So I hear," growled Daggett. "Did you know that Pirani was coming here, Paige?"

"Yes," replied Jerry. "We had an appointment for ten o'clock."

A photographer came to photograph the body just then. "We'll have to get him out of the elevator," said Daggett, "as soon as this fellow is finished. Eh, McCoy, get a stretcher and send for the police ambulance."

He stepped into the open elevator as soon as the photographer put away his camera and began to go carefully through Pirani's pockets. A handkerchief, some bills and coins were all he found until he thrust his hand into the breast pocket of Pirani's well tailored jacket. He drew forth a square case of black leather, snapped it open and there lying on the white velvet of the lining was a great glowing emerald in a sort of nest of gold links set with tiny winking diamonds.

"My God!" gasped Jerry. "Pirani had the emerald!"

Daggett snapped the case shut with a loud click and put it in his pocket.

"That emerald is mine, you know," suggested Jerry tentatively.

93

"Yes, I know," replied Daggett grimly. "If it had belonged to anyone else, it might have been stolen."

Jerry turned brick-red and the excited reporters craning their necks in the background began to scribble furiously. I wished that Daggett would be more cautious in front of the press. I saw George Cobb just coming up and making frantic signs to me.

"You take Paige back and wait in his apartment with him until I come back," commanded Daggett. "I want to talk to you both."

I took Jerry's arm and piloted him back down the hall. The reporters swarmed around, but I shoved Jerry inside the apartment and stalled off the lot outside his door, answering as few of their questions as possible, but I should be sympathetic to the boys, goodness knows. I finally turned and went back into ninety-four and slammed the door. Jerry was sitting on the couch with his head in his hands.

"Cheer up, kid," I bleated in a tone I tried to make hearty and confident. "You look as if your best friend had been killed instead of a man that you didn't like anyway."

"Yeah," gloomed Jerry. "I didn't like him anyway. I was heard to make threats about him the morning before the murder, I knew that he was coming to the apartment and waited for him at the elevator with a butcher knife. I didn't bother to steal the emerald because it was mine anyway. You heard what Daggett said. Isn't that the way he has it doped? Isn't that the way anyone would figure it? That elevator stunt too; they'll think it was someone familiar with the building and the type of car who pulled that."

Just then there was a peremptory rap and I went to the door to admit Daggett.

"Well, Paige," he began, "how about this appointment? I didn't know that you and Pirani were on calling terms."

"Pirani went to Uncle Jonathan's funeral, the services at the grave and everything and rode back from the cemetery in the family car with Aunt Agatha and me. After Aunt Agatha had left, he made the appointment. He said that he had something important to tell me, but that he couldn't come up until evening. I was expecting him at ten o'clock."

"Have you any idea what he wanted to tell you?"

"Not the faintest, unless he wanted to give me the emerald, which hardly seems likely."

"Anyone else know about this appointment?"

"Jim knew. He came over here this afternoon after the funeral. We had a couple of drinks and I told him about it and invited him to come in later and spend the night with me."

"You didn't talk to anyone else?"

"No."

"You put through a long telephone call about eight o'clock. Who was that to?"

"Celia Emory," replied Jerry with rising color.

"Did you tell her about this appointment?"

"Well, yes, I guess I did."

"The circumstances, the hour you expected him and everything?"

"Yes, but," Jerry suddenly caught the import of these questions and stopped in consternation. Daggett didn't pursue the matter. He got up and went to the folding doors of the pullman kitchenette, pushed them back and looked over the compact arrangement of stove, sink, icebox, and cupboards with a critical eye.

"Where do you keep your cutlery?" he asked.

"In that little drawer at the left," said Jerry startled.

There was a rattle of metal as Daggett fumbled in the drawer and then he drew out a big knife with a crinkled edge and a green painted handle. "Is this your bread knife?"

"Yes."

"Do these fancy green knives come with the apartment?"

"What are you driving at, Daggett?" cried Jerry.

"I asked you a question," said Daggett evenly.

"All right then. No, they don't. I bought that myself. Why?"

"Isn't there supposed to be a bread knife in the equipment furnished for cooking here?"

"Yes."

"Then why did you buy your own?"

"Because I lost the other one and didn't like to ask for another."

"How did you lose it?"

"I don't know. Probably wrapped it up with the garbage. When you try to get meals in these damn pullman kitchenettes, things are always getting mislaid and lost. The management have already provided me with three can openers. I didn't want to ask them for a new bread knife."

"How long ago did you buy this knife? It appears to be new. That green paint hasn't begun to rub off against the other utensils in the drawer yet."

"I bought it two days ago at a hardware store on Clark Street. For God's sake, Daggett, what are you driving at?" cried Jerry desperately.

"Pirani was stabbed through the heart with a bread knife with a sharp straight blade and a black wooden handle," explained Daggett dryly. "Tyson, the manager of this place, said he couldn't identify it, as he buys them wholesale by the dozen. There is supposed to be one among the cutlery in every apartment."

There was a tense silence as Daggett finished speaking. Jerry's lips twisted but he said nothing. He gave an involuntary shudder as Daggett tossed the green-handled knife back into the drawer.

"Any fingerprints?" I suggested, mostly to break that awful silence.

"No, the murderer seems to have been wearing gloves. However, Patrolman McCoy found a smear of blood on the knob of the door leading to the fire escape on this floor."

Jerry brightened a bit at this information, "I'd like to see that smear."

"Well, come on out and look at it," said Daggett. We went out to the hall where the cop called McCoy was waiting. Daggett gave him a little nod as we passed and I saw that he went on into Jerry's apartment. The poor kid's stuff was going to be pawed over again, I suspected, in a search for bloody gloves or something. That dick, Oliver, and the other cop were peering at the fire escape door at the end of the hall.

"Someone with blood on his glove turned this knob," said Oliver as we came up. "This is blood all right and it is barely dry. No fingerprints anywhere except around the elevator and there there are too many to be of any use."

"Aren't there any locks on these doors?" asked Daggett, when he had finished looking at the blood-smeared knob.

"No," replied Oliver. "They open out and are unlocked and easy to open from inside but there are no knobs outside and the door is too heavy to pry open even though it isn't locked. It would be darned hard to do even with a set of proper tools and this one hasn't been tampered with."

"That's right," said Jerry. "The people in the apartment were always going up on the roof last summer to get some cool air and then not being able to get in again from the fire escape. Sort of embarrassing too, because we aren't supposed to climb the fire escape or go up on the roof. It makes Tyson furious."

"He can't stop us this time," said Daggett and pushed open the heavy door. The chill night air flowed over us. We looked out high over Lincoln Park with its street lamps strung like a glimmering chain of jewels across the dark expanse of parkland. We could see the flash of headlights from the moving cars far below and the diffused glow of the city to the south. "You stay here and let us in when we come back," Daggett told Oliver and the cop.

The fire escape zigzagged across a vertical row of windows at the back of the apartment, cutting across them in such a way that its own iron framework acted as bars for the windows so that no one could enter the windows from the fire escape even if they were unlocked. I commented on this fact and Jerry added, "The fire escape doesn't run across the window on the top floor just above. A man could get in there if the window was unlocked."

He led us up one flight to the top floor of the apartment where the fire escape terminated in a little balcony. An iron ladder flat against the brick went on to the roof but left the upper window of the row free. There was a light in the window and the shade was not drawn, the occupants evidently feeling that since they were several stories higher than any other building in the block no one could look in. They had not reckoned with the fire escape, however, so we three men could look freely into the room in which Valerie Burke and Betty Bennett were talking earnestly. Daggett rapped on the window and both girls looked up, startled, and Valerie gave a little shriek. "Open the fire escape door and let us in," shouted Daggett. "We want to talk to you."

Betty scurried out to the hall to let the men in while Valerie arranged her negligee of pink satin and lace more becomingly on the chaise longue on which she was reclining.

"You'll have to pardon our receiving you this way," said Betty as she led us into the apartment. "But Val's had quite a shock, you know."

"You are good to let us in at all coming by way of the fire escape in the middle of the night," said Jerry. "This is Miss Burke, Inspector Daggett. She is the girl who was so frightened in the elevator."

"Yes," murmured Daggett. "Very unfortunate occurrence." But his eyes were roving around the apartment and he barely looked at the girl on the couch.

"Do you keep this window locked?" asked Daggett.

"Not always," answered Betty.

"Was it locked this evening?"

"No. Val and I were out to dinner, then I came on home when she went to the theatre. The place seemed sort of hot and stuffy when I came in, so I opened the window a bit to air out."

"Were you here during the evening?"

"No, I've been playing bridge with some friends of mine down the hall. I was there when I heard Val screaming."

"The window was open all evening then?"

"Yes, and the funny thing was that it was open a lot wider when we came back in just now. I thought I'd put it up just a crack but it was open quite wide and the place was like an icebox. It's chilly now, isn't it?"

Daggett walked over to the window. "How wide open was it when you returned?"

"About this far," said Betty indicating about eight inches on the window.

"Not enough for a man to crawl through," mused Daggett.

"Oh, no," gasped Betty. "You don't mean that you think the murderer came through our apartment?"

"Were these doors open while you were away?" Daggett continued, ignoring her startled question, and pointing to the door which opened on their pullman kitchenette like Jerry's.

"Why, yes, I guess they were," said Betty. "I opened the kitchen to get out the ice cubes. We have only single trays in the apartment iceboxes and they needed more ice at the bridge session and asked me to bring the tray from my box."

Daggett stalked over to the kitchenette and pulled open the drawer which held the cutlery. "Have you a breadknife, Miss Bennett?" he asked, after poking about in the drawer.

"Why, I don't know; I guess so."

"I don't see one here," said Daggett.

"Maybe we never had one. Breakfast is the only meal we eat in, and then we only have coffee and orange jucie and rye krisp. We never buy bread; it's too fattening."

"How long have you lived here?"

"Just a couple of weeks. We moved in when Val signed on with Balaban and Katz. She dances in the ballet at the Roosevelt."

"Jim," said Daggett, "will you go down and send Oliver up? I want

97

to check the window and the cupboard drawer for fingerprints. You'll probably find him in Ninety-four."

"Yes, I know," I said. "Good night, ladies."

"Good night," chorused the girls.

"So Oliver is down in my apartment," muttered Jerry as we went down the stairs," looking for bloody gloves and gory breadknives I suppose. Well, thank God, he won't find any."

We entered the apartment, sent Oliver on his errand and sat wearily down.

"Well, we can now cross Pirani off the list of suspects," sighed Jerry.

"Not necessarily," I reminded him. "Just because somebody knifed him tonight doesn't mean that he couldn't have been poisoning someone else last night."

"You don't think that the same person is responsible for both murders then?"

"I don't know. Poisoners don't usually resort to steel, but this was an emergency. It takes time and planning to administer poison. I can't see the motive of any one individual for bumping off both of them, however. The emerald was the only thing the two victims had in common."

"They were both related to Aunt Agatha," put in Jerry.

"Well, doesn't look as if we could settle it tonight. How about a drink? Got any more of that whiskey?"

"No, sorry; I finished it off this evening waiting for Pirani."

"There's still my wine; how about a swig of that? I need a bracer and it doesn't look as if I'd get much sleep tonight either."

"Are you going out again?" asked Jerry.

"I want to keep a tail on Daggett, if I can; he may unearth something tonight. This second murder with the first still unsolved is going to put him on his mettle," I said opening up the kitchenette doors and retrieving the brown bundle from the shelf. I tore off the wrappings carelessly, then suddenly stiffened to attention.

"Jerry," I cried, "look at this bottle!" I held it up, a flattened bottle made of green frosted glass.

"Why, it's just like Uncle's tonic bottle. Where did you say you got it?"

"From Dan Murphy who lives in the alley back of the Cranes'. Wait 'til I show Daggett."

I ran out in the hall where a policeman was leaning against the wall near the elevator smoking a cigar. "Has Inspector Daggett come down yet?" I asked.

"Yeah," replied the cop. "He's gone, him and Detective Oliver went about five minutes ago. I'm in charge. What you want?"

"Nothing," said I and returned to the apartment. "He's given me the slip, thereby missing one of the best clues we've found so far. That's his tough luck."

"Where are you going?" asked Jerry, as I started scrambling into my coat.

"I'm going to see Dan Murphy," said I.

"I'll go with you," said Jerry. "I can't stay here alone."

But the policeman stationed by the elevator put out a detaining hand as Jerry came down the hall.

"Hey, where do you think you are going?" he said gruffly, snatching Jerry's arm. "I got orders to bring you down to the station for questioning as soon as the chief calls in."

Jerry gave me a despairing look. "I guess I'm not going. Are they going to keep me there all night?" he asked the cop.

"I dunno," he answered casually. "I just got orders to bring you down."

"What does that mean, do you suppose?" said Jerry, looking at me with a white face and twitching lips. "Is Daggett arresting me for this murder?"

"Oh, no," I answered as cheerfully as possible. "It's just a formality. I don't believe that he'd have a warrant for your arrest."

"You come back here tonight even if I have to spend the night in the pen. I'll leave a key at the desk. So long and good luck."

"Good luck yourself," I replied, thinking that the poor lad needed it; things were looking dark for him. I had to take one thing at a time, however. That blood smear on the fire escape would keep Daggett from making any formal charges against Jerry at the present and what I wanted to know most was where Dan Murphy got that flat green bottle.

CHAPTER 15

THE little house in the alley was dark and still when I groped my way to its door. My vigorous pounding at first brought no response and I was beginning to think that perhaps Dan was still at his shop, though it was almost midnight, when I heard a snort and a growl and a creaking bed spring and then a gruff voice calling, "Who is it?"

"It's me, Jim McBride, Dan. Let me in. I've got to see you about something important."

The light went on and presently Danny threw open the door. "Well," he said, giving me a cheerful lopsided grin, "didn't expect you back so soon. Don't tell me I got to sleep in the Morris chair again tonight."

"No, I didn't come to ask for a bed. Sorry to rout you out but I had to ask you something that wouldn't wait 'til morning." I tore the wrappings from the bundle I carried and held out for Dan's inspection his own offering of that morning. "Where did you get this bottle?"

"Why, I dunno. I just picked it up somewhere. I told you I sort of collect 'em to bottle off my stuff in. What's the big idea?"

"See if you can't remember where you found this particular one. It's an unusual bottle. Haven't you any recollection about it?" I begged, desperate both from fatigue and urgency.

Dan took the bottle and squinted at it speculatively. "Sure, I recollect now," he said. "I picked it out of an ashcan in the alley on my way to work. I saw it sticking up out of the can and thought it was a nice color and a good shape to carry, being flat like this, so I pulled it out and put it in my pocket."

"What day was that?"

"Let's see, day before yesterday, Wednesday morning, because it was Tuesday it snowed, wasn't it, and there was still snow in the alley that morning."

"Do you remember whose ashcan it was?"

"It was right along here in this block. I guess maybe it was Graysons'."

"Not Cranes'?"

"No."

"Was there anything in the bottle?"

"No, it was empty, been washed out, but I washed it again, of course, before I filled it."

"Was there a label on it?"

"Yeah, come to think of it there was, a druggist's label with some writing but it had got all smeared when the bottle was washed I guess and I couldn't read it. Don't know that I tried very hard."

"What became of the label?"

"Why, it come off when I washed the bottle. I suppose I threw it away. I don't remember."

"Where did you wash the bottle?"

"In the sink over at my shop. I picked it up on my way to work see, real early, 'bout six-thirty it was. I had some things I wanted to do before the shop got busy. I see this bottle sticking out of the ashcan. I'm sure it was Graysons' more I think of it, because the Cranes' can stands inside their back gate by the garage and the Graysons don't have any back fence; their can just sits in the alley. The bottle had been wrapped in newspaper but the wind or maybe some of the dogs or cats that prowl around this neighborhood must have loosened the wrapping, 'cause it was sticking out of the paper. I put it in my overcoat pocket like I told you and went on over to the shop. That evening when things was kinda slack, I happened to remember about it; fished it outa my pocket to look at it, washed it out and put it in my pocket again to bring home."

"Did you have it with you when you picked me up last night?"

"Yeah. And when I was gonna give you some wine, I used this 'cause I thought it would be a good size and shape for you to carry."

"Had any more burglaries?"

"Nope. Rummy thing, wasn't it? Getting my shack and my shop both broke into within twelve hours, and nothing particular took."

"The bottle was at the shop then during the day when your house was ransacked and was at the house during the night when the shop was broken into, that right?"

"Sure, but— Say, what is this about that bottle anyway? You meaning to say that a guy would risk breaking into a place just to get a green glass bottle?"

"That's what I'm wondering too," said I. "Do you think there's any chance of locating that label if we went over to the shop right away?"

"I dunno. It might still be in the wastebasket over there. I ain't emptied it."

"Will you take me over there?"

"Sure," said Dan, still mystified, but catching some of my excitement. "As soon as I can get my pants on."

Dan struggled into his clothes while I paced restlessly up and down. "Let's get going and bring a flashlight if you have one. I'd like you to show me where you found the bottle."

"Okay, old-timer. Let's shove off."

We started down the dark, deserted mews. Dan flashed his light and caught a baleful green shimmer as a sleek, well fed black monster crossed our path.

"That's Crane's cat," chuckled Dan. "Going home from a wild night."

"Yes, he's probably been indulging in nameless orgies on somebody's back fence and will go home and purr on a cushion in Agatha Crane's boudoir looking sweet and innocent as you please."

"Yeah, cats is sneaky, two-faced critters. I like dogs. They're honest anyway. There's the can, this one here." He turned his flash on a battered can with a lopsided cover. "You'd think these rich guys could afford better garbage cans, wouldn't you? The cover was off the morning I took the bottle out."

"You could stand in the Cranes' yard and toss a package into the can easily enough if the cover was off," I mused.

"Sure, easy," agreed Dan.

I didn't pursue the subject and we walked in silence down the alley and then cut over to Clark Street. Dan's shop was a little hole-in-the-wall with a green painted door and a single window in which were rows of pulp magazines with lurid covers, an array of pipes, of Yo-yos and puzzle games—you know the sort of little shop I mean.

Dan whipped out his key and unlocked the door. "Everything ship-shape tonight," he said, as he turned on the switch and took a quick glance around the crowded little shop.

He led the way to the back of the shop where, behind a sagging monk's cloth curtain, was a stained washbowl with a single faucet. "Here's where I washed the bottle," said Dan. "If the label didn't go down the sink, it ought to be in that basket there."

He pointed to a green-painted tin container which I was delighted to see piled high with crumpled pieces of wrapping paper. I scouted around at the back of the shop for an empty carton, placed it beside

101

the wastebasket and then settled down to the job of methodically transferring all the odds and ends from the wastebasket to the carton. Dan squatted down to help as soon as he got the idea and for a few minutes there was no sound but the rustling of paper as we worked intently at our task. In a very short time there was nothing left in the tin basket but cigarette ashes and a few cooky crumbs, the carton was full and there was no sign of the missing label.

"Maybe the burglar found it," suggested Dan.

"I doubt it; he probably thinks it is still on the bottle. That is why he is so anxious to get it back. We went through this stuff kind of fast. Let's try once more." And again we started the transfer, this time from the carton to the basket.

"What ho!" cried Dan suddenly as he smoothed a crumpled piece of wrapping paper with his huge paw. "Here she is."

Stuck to the creased brown surface was a druggist's label, its corners torn, the ink streaked and smeared, but otherwise a facsimile of the one that I had seen on that other green bottle in the table drawer of ¬Jonathan Crane's desk.

"That's it all right," I cried jubilantly. "What a piece of luck! How'd it get stuck on here?"

"It was wet when I threw it in and there musta been enough glue left on it so it stuck to this paper and got crumpled up with it so we missed it going through the first time."

It pulled away from the wrapping paper easily enough since the glue was pretty well gone from the label. I took it over nearer the light to examine it more closely. In a few places the paper was scraped as if someone had hurriedly tried to remove the label with a knife or finger nail, found it too tightly stuck and given up the job.

"Try this, professor," said Dan, offering me a reading glass which he had taken from one of his stock cases. It helped a lot.

"This top line says Jonathan Crane all right, then there's the doctor's name, but it's most scraped off, and the date. That's October, as I live. This must be the first tonic bottle that Mrs. Bruns said was thrown out several weeks ago."

"Well, I'm glad you found it and no doubt it is the first tonic bottle, though I'll be blowed if I can see why that's anything to get a feller out of bed and out in the cold midnight about. You knew old Crane was taking a tonic, eh, and was on his second bottle. What's all the excitement?"

"It's sort of complicated to explain now. You'd better cut along home and take up your sleeping where I interrupted you. Sorry I had to drag you out like this, and it may turn out to be nothing but a wild goose chase after all."

"It looks that way to me," said Dan, "but that's all right. Glad to oblige. Cheerio, and you'd better be gettin' some sleep yourself."

I quite agreed with him. Now that the excitement of my discovery had died down, exhaustion was overtaking me again. Dan plodded off toward Astor Street and I hailed a cab on a Clark Street corner.

"Has Mr. Paige come in yet?" I asked the clerk in the lobby of the Surf Street apartment.

"No, he hasn't," he replied. It was the same fellow who had lost the elevator earlier in the evening. "Say, he went off in a car with a couple of cops. Do you think he's been arrested for that Italian guy's murder?"

"Did he leave a key for me?" I wasn't discussing Jerry with the night clerk.

"Yeah, here it is." He held it out with an injured look, snubbed.

I went up to the empty apartment. The thought of Jerry and what might be happening to him depressed me. I tried to put a call through to Daggett. He was out but I got in touch with Oliver and asked him if anything important had turned up. He told me that he and Daggett had gone over to the Crane house and had interviewed Mrs. Crane and the servants.

"Glean anything?"

"Nothing much. They all claimed to have been right in the house all evening except Violet and that chauffeur. They went to a movie together, one on Chicago Avenue where they were well known, the ticket-taker remembered them so I guess that was straight enough."

"How about Jerry?" I asked. "Is he still down there?"

"I don't know. Daggett seems leery of arresting him just yet. He looks guilty as hell, but he's too well connected to be clapping any false arrest, but they put him through a course of sprouts."

I turned away from the phone, dug a pair of pajamas from the bottom drawer of Jerry's bureau, pulled his rollaway bed from its niche in the wall. I had just climbed into bed, careful to keep one side unrumpled in case Jerry returned and was soothing myself with a last cigarette when I heard a key in the lock and in walked Jerry himself. He looked white and tired.

"Gosh, I'm glad to see you!" I cried. "How are things?"

"Nothing new that I know of," he answered wearily, "but then I've been answering questions, not asking them. I'm done in, but anyway they didn't lock me up for the night, that's something. How about you? Did you find anything?"

"Well, I got what I went after. What do you make of that?" I pointed to the green bottle on the bedside table.

Jerry, in the process of untying his shoes looked up at the bottle with a languid eye.

"What is it? That homemade wine you've been trying to pawn off on me all evening?"

"Right, and here's the label that was on it, a bit smeared but still legible. Notice the date."

"Well, he had used up one bottle of the stuff, you know. This must be the first bottle. What's so exciting about that?"

"Mrs. Bruns said the first bottle was thrown out several weeks ago. My friend picked this one out of the Graysons' ashcan Wednesday morning."

"Maybe she was just careless and didn't get around to it before."

"Someone has been trying very hard to get this bottle back. Dan's house was ransacked during the day on Wednesday while he had the bottle at the shop and his shop was broken into at night when the bottle was at his house. At least that's the way I dope it out. It looks as if someone wanted this bottle and wanted it bad."

"But why?"

"Because it had contained poison and if that was discovered, it spoiled someone's alibi."

"How do you know there was poison in it?"

"I don't, that's just the trouble. I haven't had the contents analyzed and while I'm taking no chances on drinking it myself, I am afraid there isn't much possibility that there are any traces of strophanthus in this bottle. Dan washed it out."

"Why are you so steamed up about it then? It doesn't change things any," said Jerry wearily.

"But it does," I insisted. "The fact that there were two tonic bottles exactly alike except for the date on the label in the Crane house the night of November 12, means that the bottle we found in the library desk the next morning was not necessarily the bottle from which Jonathan Crane poured out his medicine. It might have been that bottle right there on the table. Crane would never have noticed that the label was dated earlier. Later the new innocuous bottle could have been substituted and this one thrown out in the ashcan. Though why leave it in the ashcan, if it was so important?"

I stopped to ponder this question, but Jerry's eyes suddenly lit up as the real implication of my find dawned on him. "That means, then, that the person who poisoned Uncle was not necessarily in the house at the time he drank the medicine. It could all have been planted ahead of time."

"Sure, it could have been done by anyone who had access to that library drawer before and after Jonathan Crane drank his medicine last Tuesday night."

"Gosh, that does make a difference," mused Jerry.

"Yeah, but we'd better turn in. We're both dead and there's lots to do tomorrow. I feel as if I could sleep for a week but you'd better set the alarm for 7:30."

Jerry undressed, set the alarm and crawled into bed beside me. "Tomorrow will be a better day," I assured him.

CHAPTER 16

W E WERE wakened suddenly out of deep sleep to the shrill jangle of a bell. Half drunk with slumber, Jerry sat up with his eyes still shut, stretched out a practiced arm, caught up the alarm clock, pushed the switch over and flopped back upon the pillows, but the bell went right on ringing. I blinked and looked at the clock. The hands pointed to seven minutes of seven.

"It is'nt the clock, it's the telephone," I grumbled and climbed wearily out of bed shivering in the chill blast from the open window.

"Hello," I called into the instrument in a hoarse, morning voice. "Hello," responded an unfamiliar male voice over the wire, "I want to talk to James McBride."

"You are talking to him," I answered. "Who are you?"

"Well, my name is Emil Holtzwarth, but it doesn't matter much because you don't know me anyway. I'm a milkman."

"I see. Well, I don't need any milk this morning, Emil."

"I know, but it isn't about milk. I got a message for you and the young lady says it is urgent."

"Young lady? What young lady?"

"Well, I don't know, and maybe she ain't even young, but I just thought she might be and she signed the note in the cream bottle 'Violet'."

"What note? What are you talking about? Where are you anyway?"

"I'm downstairs. I'm through with my milk route and I drove over this way before I turned the wagon in."

"Well, come on upstairs and explain. We aren't dressed but that doesn't matter. It's room 94."

"All right, I'll be up," said the milkman.

"For the love of Pete, who are you inviting up to my apartment at this hour of the morning?" grumbled Jerry.

"A milkman named Holtzwarth. He says he found a note in a cream bottle signed 'Violet'. I don't know what it's all about, but I thought I'd better have him up and find out. You'll have to stay in bed because I'm going to wear your bathrobe," I added, retrieving that object from the closet and wrapping it around me.

On the threshold stood a swarthy young fellow in a uniform with a white cap and black visor. "I'm Emil Holtzwarth," he said.

"Glad to meet you; I'm Jim McBride," I responded, sliding back the over-long sleeve of Jerry's bathrobe so that I could shake hands.

"Now, what is all this about a note?"

"Well, you see, I have a milk route along Astor Street and this morning when I took the order into the Crane house, you know, the place where the old gent was poisoned—"

"Yes, yes, I know, go on," I said impatiently.

"Well, I left the milk and cream that they'd marked on the milk card and then I gathered up the empty bottles and was going away when I saw a cream bottle lying on the ground near the back steps and it had a piece of paper in it. I thought maybe it was a special order for me so I picked it up and fished out this paper."

He drew a folded sheet of paper from his pocket and handed it to me. The note was scrawled in pencil in a slanting feminine hand on a sheet of cheap notepaper and read:

Dear Milkman:

Will you please get a message to Jim McBride? He is a columnist on the *Leader* and he lives in Oak Park. Tell him that Violet is in danger. I've got to get away from here. I am scared.

Violet.

I read this hasty, enigmatic message with a cold fear gripping my heart, then handed it over to Jerry in silence. I had a sudden vivid recollection of the wide-eyed terror on Violet's little pointed face when I had told her to call on me if she needed help and to watch her step in the Crane house because the murderer was still abroad. I hadn't been very serious at the time but apparently my warning was more to the point than I had imagined.

One glance at the note brought Jerry up from his pillows with a wild light in his amber eyes. "My God! what can have happened now? It sounds serious; we've got to get over there right away. The kid may really be in danger."

Jerry jumped from his bed, slammed it back up into the wall, rumpled bedclothes and all, with one impatient shove and reached for his clothes.

"What time did you find this note?" I asked, as I pulled on my socks.

"It wasn't quite six, I guess," replied Emil Holtzwarth who had been watching us with popeyed excitement and confusion. "I had to wait until I could get to a telephone. I stopped at a drugstore that was open over on Goethe Street and I called the newspaper first and they gave me your Oak Park number and I called there and finally a lady answered and said you were spending the night here. It wasn't so far over to Surf Street and my route took me on north anyway, so I decided I'd better deliver the note in person. It was so early yet I knew nobody'd be up and I thought perhaps the note was just a joke or something."

"I don't think anyone in that house is in a mood for jokes, you couldn't tell how long the bottle had been lying there, I suppose?"

"Not exactly, but I think it must have been there all night because it was stuck in the frost. It was lying on its side and it was cracked a bit too as if it had been thrown out of a window."

This sounded even more ominous. Violet must be a prisoner in that house. But why? She must have stumbled upon information which made her a menace to the murderer. If that mysterious individual had already killed two persons, a third would not make much difference, I

106

thought with a shudder.

"Gee, I didn't realize it was anything as bad as this," gasped the milkman. "Maybe I should have gone in myself, right then."

"No, you did very well, thanks," I said absently. I went to the phone and tried to get a call through to Daggett, but couldn't reach him. I didn't have time to pursue the matter so I left word that Jerry and I had gone to the Crane house on urgent business. That ought to bring him around.

"Do you want me to go back there with you?" asked the milkman timidly. "I'd like to help if I could. Violet is Mrs. Crane's maid, isn't she? I wish I could meet her."

"You'd better take your horse home. You can meet Violet later," I returned impatiently. The milkman sighed with suppressed emotion. This had been a thrilling morning for him, no doubt, but Jerry and I hustled him downstairs as soon as we had completed our hurried ablutions and dressing, sent him on his way with his milk wagon and hailed a cab. Virtue finally responded to our insistent ringing of the Crane's front doorbell, and looked out with a disgruntled stare upon such early and inconvenient callers. "Good morning," he said with reluctant dignity. "Will you step in?"

"We want to see Violet," said Jerry.

Virtue stared at him with astonishment and disapproval. "Violet isn't up yet. Mrs. Crane gave orders that Violet was not to be disturbed this morning as she had been ill last evening and had taken a sleeping tablet. I was just preparing to take Mrs. Crane's breakfast up myself since—"

"Where is Violet's room" shouted Jerry and dashed for the stairs, without waiting for an answer. I followed him. "Sleeping tablet!" Perhaps we were too late after all. It didn't seem like Agatha Crane to administer sleeping powders and permit her servants to sleep overtime.

"The servants' rooms are all on the third floor," Jerry flung at me over his shoulder, as he rushed through the second floor hall. All the doors were closed and there was no sound. We made little noise ourselves as we fled along the thickly carpeted hall to the rear stairs that led to the servants' floor. Virtue was now panting along behind us.

Jerry reached the head of the stairs first and flung open the first door he came to. He looked in upon a square room, neat and orderly with the exception of the unmade bed in the corner.

"That's my room," panted Virtue. "Briscombe's is opposite and that next one is Violet's."

I slid past and tried the handle of Violet's door. It was locked. I banged on it. There was a moment of silence in which I had a horrid, chilling remembrance of that "sleeping powder." Had the message come too late after all? I rapped again, louder and more insistently and to my great relief a weak voice quavered from the other side of the door, "Who's there?"

"It's Jim and Jerry. I got the message you left in the cream bottle and came as soon as I could. Are you all right?"

"Yes, I guess so, but be careful. Don't talk so loud."

"I can't whisper through the door. May I come in?"

"Not unless you have the key." There was the trace of an hysterical giggle in Violet's voice.

"You mean you are locked in?"

"Yes."

"Who did it? Who has the key now?"

"I—I don't know." A note of terror and uncertainty had crept into her tone again.

"You must know who locked you in," I said, rattling the door handle impatiently.

There was a frightened gasp from within, but no reply. I realized that someone had instilled a dread into Violet's gentle soul which even my reassuring presence did not allay. There was no use trying to press her for details, at least from the other side of the door.

"Can you get a key to this door?" I demanded, turning to Virtue, who had been standing by, open-mouthed.

"I don't know, sir," he stammered. "There is no master key for the rooms on this floor, but perhaps my key would fit. These are ordinary locks."

He pulled a bunch of keys from his pocket and began trying them in the lock with no success. I tried the door across the hall. It was open and there was a key in the lock on the inside. I pulled it out and handed it to Virtue.

"That is Mrs. Bruns' room. She's downstairs cooking breakfast. None of the keys fit, sir. I don't understand this at all. Who could have wanted to lock Violet in her room?"

"You didn't hear any quarrel or struggle or anything of the sort last night?" I asked, ignoring his question.

"No, sir. The police came and asked us all questions and we were all upset about that, of course, but everything was very quiet after they left. Violet didn't bang on her door or ask to be let out. I should have heard that, I'm sure."

"Where is Briscombe?"

"I don't know. I haven't seen him this morning. That is his door there. He's probably still in bed."

I thought this extremely unlikely but I said nothing and tried the door. It was locked. There was no answer to my banging. If the fellow had been there, he would surely have heard the commotion in the hall and have come out before this. I was suddenly so concerned as to the whereabouts of Briscombe that Violet's predicament no longer seemed very important.

Just then there was a long peal of the doorbell. "I bet that's Daggett," I said. "You stay here, Jerry, and I'll go down and let him in." And I started down the stairs two at a time. I heard a murmur of voices from behind a closed door on the second floor but I was too excited to stop. It was Daggett as I had supposed, looking pretty grim. There was a squad car outside too. It seemed the house was being watched and he'd been tipped off of our arrival.

"What's up?" he snapped.

"I don't quite know," I answered breathlessly. "I got an SOS from Violet sent via the milkman and Jerry and I rushed over here. Violet's locked in her room. Have you a master key?"

"Yeah," said Daggett and followed me upstairs.

This key worked and we flung back the door. Violet was sitting hunched up on the side of her crumpled bed. She had evidently slept in her uniform and had slept badly, for it was rumpled and twisted about her slender figure.

"Violet! What has happened?" I cried going to her and taking one of her hands reassuringly. "Are you all right?"

"Yes," she breathed.

"Who locked you in here?" I asked for the second time.

"B-briscombe did," she whispered with an apprehensive glance about her.

"Why?" I pursued.

"Be-because he was 'fraid I would tell someone that he wasn't with me at the movie last night. He took me in but he went out the rear exit during the show and he didn't come back again. I went home alone but he said he'd kill me if I told. You won't leave me here alone again, will you?"

"No," I assured her. Just then I saw Daggett making a dive for the stairs. I dropped Violet's hand and started after him. "You stay with Violet, Jerry," I shouted as I rushed after him.

Just as Daggett and I rounded the turn of the stairs we saw the door to the right of the stairway open cautiously and then swiftly close as the person within became aware of footsteps on the stair. Daggett plunged into the room, with me behind him.

It was the boudoir of Agatha Crane. That lady, her voluptuous person again swathed in the gilt-stenciled black velvet robe was lying on a chaise longue upholstered in gold satin. Standing stiffly at the foot of her couch was Briscombe with his back to the door. They both gave the appearance of having been engaged in a formal conversation, but we knew that one of them had tried to leave the room a few moments before. Briscombe turned and looked at us in apparent surprise while Mrs. Crane cried indignantly, "Gentlemen, this is a most unwarranted intrusion. You might at least have knocked."

Briscombe glared at us and then bowed to his mistress. "If that is all, madame, I beg you to excuse me," he said stiffly. I was suddenly aware that Briscombe was no longer in uniform. It is usually disillusioning to see a handsome chauffeur in his civilian garb but Briscombe looked, if anything, even more distinguished in the well cut dark blue suit he was wearing.

"Very well, Briscombe, you may go," said Mrs. Crane with a dignified gesture of dismissal.

"Stay where you are, Briscombe," ordered Daggett. "Why did you lock Violet in her room last night?"

"That is a little personal matter between her and me," said Briscombe.

"Where did you go last night after you left Violet in the movie theatre?" demanded Daggett grimly.

His eyes were fixed upon Briscombe with a relentless gaze, but I knew Briscombe's poker face would reveal nothing and turned my attention instead upon Agatha Crane. The anxious look that came into her sapphire eyes, her involuntary gesture of tenderness and dismay as Daggett put this question, her pale, parted lips told their story and a flash of intuition came to me, the one solution which would give logic to this crazy puzzle.

"I was with Violet in the theatre until we came back here together," said Briscombe.

"John Briscombe, you are under arrest for the murder of Benedetto Montebruzzi."

"And Jonathan Crane," I added.

"You can't arrest me for murder on the whim of that silly girl," cried Briscombe. Violet was right, he did have hot, terrifying eyes. "And I wasn't in the house at the time that Jonathan Crane drank that poison. You know that!" He glared at me.

"I know you weren't," I said, "but you had plenty of time to switch Mr. Crane's harmless bottle of tonic for a poisoned one Tuesday morning, while you were supposed to be polishing that brass fender in the library. And when you came in Tuesday night after the rest of the house had gone to bed, it was easy to slip into the library and change the bottles again, and to dump the old one into the neighbor's ashcan. And you know, Briscombe, that trick of going to the library in your stocking feet and then getting back into your purposely muddied boots so you'd leave footprints to show that you had gone directly upstairs was just a bit too clever. It was the first thing that made me suspect you because there was no reason to trample in the mud in the back yard unless you had a reason for it."

"I don't know what you are talking about," snarled Briscombe. "This talk of bottles and ashcans and stocking feet means nothing to me. What did I have to gain by Jonathan Crane's death?"

"Plenty, Juliano Montebruzzi," I flung at him. This was a random shot, but it struck home. There was a moment of tense silence. Then with a little moan Agatha Crane fell back upon her luxurious couch in a dead faint. Briscombe in one swift movement was on his knees beside her, chafing her limp hands.

Daggett for once was nearly bowled over with surprise. "Where'd you get all this?" he demanded.

"I got wise to the bottle business last night and tried to get in touch with you, but couldn't. The other was just a shot in the dark."

Into this tense atmosphere came Jerry and Violet. She was looking neat and smooth again, although pale and nervous. When she saw the couple at the chaise longue, she stopped in astonishment. Then with a little gasp of sympathy she ran over to Agatha Crane's well stocked dressing table, picked up an enameled bottle of smelling salts and approached her unconscious mistress with a terrified side glance at Briscombe. He rose and moved away without looking at her, and Violet waved the bottle under Agatha Crane's nose.

The woman gave a long sigh of returning consciousness, then started up suddenly with a wild cry of "Juliano!"

"Steady, Agatha!" murmured Briscombe. Agatha Crane looked at him with a lost and terrified expression. Then as remembrance flooded over her, she buried her face in her white beautifully manicured hand and began to sob bitterly.

Briscombe looked at her with hopeless tenderness, then turned to Daggett and said quietly, "The game is finished. I am beaten. I confess to the murder of Jonathan Crane and Benedetto Montebruzzi, but I planned and executed both murders entirely alone. Agatha Crane had no foreknowledge of my plans and was in no sense an accessory. You must believe that."

"You are Juliano Montebruzzi, Mrs. Crane's first husband?"

"Yes," replied Briscombe, "but Agatha genuinely believed me to be dead when she married Crane. I had been reported dead during the war and for reasons of my own, I allowed my family to go on thinking I had been killed. Agatha married Crane in good faith. My return was a shock to her. I should never have entered her life again, I see that now. But I found her again, we discovered that we still loved each other and I believed that if I could get rid of Crane we could start over again."

"Is this true, Mrs. Crane?" asked Daggett.

"Yes," breathed Agatha, "but I did not dream that Juliano would do anything so reckless."

"Agatha loved me and she did not love Crane," continued Briscombe. "I have never been a man to accept defeat when there was a way out, even if a reckless one. Crane was old and had a weak heart, but he might have kept us apart for years. I hoped that he would be found dead in his bed and that I need never tell Agatha that I had killed him. My plans miscarried, as you know."

"Why did you kill Benedetto Montebruzzi?"

Briscombe's face darkened with anger. "Because he was trying to blackmail Agatha. There would have been no peace or safety for us while he lived and threatened us with exposure. My only chance was to kill him. I knew it was risky, but there was nothing else to do and I'm not sorry. This is the end of the Montebruzzis. Perhaps there is something in that superstition about the emerald, after all."

"What made you use an apartment breadknife to stab your cousin?"

A grim smile twitched at the corner of Briscombe's mouth. "I happened to see it lying in the drawer when I went through that top floor apartment. I had a gun and a dagger too, but I feared that the revolver would make too much noise and that I had better use a knife. My own was apt to be recognized while the other would be identified as belonging to the house and distract attention from me."

"You didn't have anyone particular in mind, did you?" sneered

111

Jerry, the memory of Daggett's comments on his new green breadknife still bitter in his mind.

Briscombe shrugged without replying or even glancing in Jerry's direction. "I took a chance, of course," he went on. "That breadknife was a clumsy weapon, my own dagger would have been safer and truer, but it has the Montebruzzi seal upon it and would have made a fine clue if I had had to leave it behind. You can see that for yourself."

He slipped his hand inside his coat and drew forth a slim shining poignard with an engraved silver hilt. A swift or furtive movement would have put us on guard, but he handled the weapon so casually and deliberately and held it out for our inspection with such an innocent gesture, as if he had drawn forth a grandfather's watch for us to look at, that we all merely stared at it curiously. Then Daggett leapt forward with a sudden exclamation, but he was too late. Briscombe, with a sudden swift skillful movement had plunged the dagger deep into his heart.

"I'm sorry, Agatha," he murmured and fell at her feet.

Daggett and I never heard the whole story of Briscombe and his strange impersonation. His lips were sealed forever; Benedetto Montebruzzi would do no explaining ever again and Agatha Crane was too broken to talk coherently in response to a leading question.

However, from Agatha, from Violet and from putting two and two together on our own, we finally assembled a fairly complete picture of the events and motives which had led up to the tragedy of the Montebruzzis. I give it to you in coherent chronological form, not the broken bits and hints from which we assembled it.

Juliano Montebruzzi and Agatha Jackson met in Rome the spring that he was twenty and she eighteen. She was an American girl traveling with her mother, he an Italian nobleman recently returned from college in England. His mother was an Englishwoman and he had been educated largely in Britain. The two young people met at a ball. In one of the intermissions Juliano took Agatha off to see the Coliseum by moonlight and that is how it started.

Both the lovers were fatherless and neither mother opposed the match since each was misinformed. Mrs. Jackson was thrilled to have her daughter marry into a noble house; she knew about the title but she did not know that the Montebruzzi estates were mortgaged and the family bankrupt.

What the Montebruzzis did not know was that, although the Jacksons, mother and daughter, were elegantly turned out in newly purchased Paris gowns and had a suite at the best hotel in Rome, that this extravagance was merely a front designed to impress eligible young men and that Mrs. Jackson was blowing all the late lamented Mr. Jackson's insurance money on this little spree.

The couple married first and got their mutual disillusionment later. They were genuinely in love but they were both young and spoiled and disappointed and their domestic bliss started under an economic

112

cloud. Then the war came along. Juliano went away leaving his young bride in the mouldy old *palazzo* with her disgruntled mother-in-law. Agatha's baby died at birth. Juliano got leavè and rushed home to comfort her, but she did nothing but berate him with the accusation that if she hadn't had to have her baby in that filthy old castle, it would have lived. The next time the young husband got leave, he found Agatha brazenly entertaining an American officer in the *palazzo*. There was a violent scene with many hard words on both sides.

A few months after he returned from this unfortunate visit to his home, he was reported missing and then dead. He was fed up with the poverty and bickering of the Palazzo Montebruzzi and being a thoroughly selfish person just decided to chuck it all. He knew that his wife and relatives believed him dead and determining to let well enough alone, he shipped for South America under an assumed name, passing himself off as an Englishman.

Juliano did pretty well for himself in South America and later drifted up to California. There he had a run of bad luck. He had heard that his wife had married a wealthy Chicagoan and when he found himself broke and stranded one day in Utah, he spent all he had left on a ticket to Chicago.

Agatha was startled, to put it mildly, when the specter of her dead husband was ushered into her Astor Street drawing room one afternoon by Virtue. When she realized that he was very much alive and no apparition she was hardly less upset, for his existence imperiled her safe comfortable position in Chicago society. Juliano assured her that he meant her no harm but that he was broke and wouldn't mind accepting a loan.

It just happened that Agatha had advertised for a new chauffeur at that time, Virtue had supposed when he showed Juliano in that he was applying for the position, and Agatha suggested that he take the position for the time being until she could figure out a way to help him. As a matter of fact, when she found that Juliano was not planning to blackmail her or destroy her position, she found his company extremely pleasant. He was still attractive, and Agatha was bored and restless after six years of marriage to an old gentleman who was for the most part indifferent to her charms. Time had softened the bitterness of those early years and the old attraction flared up between them.

Juliano was a good man with a car and settled into his life as chauffeur very easily. The long afternoon drives gave him and Agatha opportunity for long tete-a-tetes. Juliano convinced her, however, that it would divert suspicion from their intimacy if he were to indulge in a mild flirtation with Violet.

Naturally enough, Agatha and Juliano did not long remain satisfied with this arrangement. They couldn't help thinking how smooth and happy their lives would be if only old Jonathan were out of the way. Agatha couldn't divorce him and marry Juliano again because legal proceedings might have disclosed the fact that the divorce was unnecessary and besides they needed Crane's money; they both had extravagant tastes.

They talked of this just as lovers discuss some delightful but unattainable desire, but to Juliano's ruthless mind it didn't seem so unattainable. He knew the old man had a weak heart and he started reading up on cardiac poisons in the library in his odd moments. He salvaged the first tonic bottle when Mrs. Bruns threw it out and bided his time, saying nothing to Agatha. He planned to tell her only after they had found the old gent dead in his bed in the morning. Then together they could pass off his death as heart failure and prevent an autopsy.

Benedetto's appearance upon the scene complicated things considerably. He and Juliano had recognized each other at the dance with Violet. Benedetto had been sure, when he grasped this situation, that he could blackmail Agatha into returning the emerald necklace, and he was horribly distressed when he discovered that Crane had given it to another woman and that it had really got away from him. He took the Montebruzzi superstition with all seriousness and, I confess, the tragedies which followed the selling of the emerald almost made one believe in its evil propensities.

Juliano's plan had become doubly dangerous with Benedetto on the scene but he was unwilling to turn back. On that fatal Tuesday when he was supposedly scouring the brass in the library, he had substituted the first tonic bottle with the strophanthus addition for the harmless second bottle in the library table drawer. When he returned to the house that night after driving Jerry to his apartment, and found everything dark and quiet, he naturally surmised that all had gone well. He took off his shoes at the back door, tiptoed into the library and quietly switched the bottles again, dumped the other one in the neighbor's ashcan, planning to retrieve it and destroy it in the morning, and then walked upstairs in his carefully muddied boots leaving a clear track from the back door up the servants' stairs, to show, in case the matter should be in question, that he had gone directly to his room on entering the house. It was those unnecessarily muddy tracks which had aroused my suspicions on that first morning that I had stepped out into the otherwise clean, empty kitchen.

You know already how sadly Juliano's well laid plans went awry. Instead of going to his room, Jonathan Crane went unexpectedly out into the night and when Juliano arose the next morning, the police were already in the house, the autopsy was performed, the bottle was gone from the ashcan and worst of all, there was Benedetto slyly holding the key to the mystery.

Agatha suspected immediately what had happened, although Juliano did not find time to tell her everything until later in the day. He had to confess about Benedetto also, for that wily young man began blackmail threats immediately. That was his message the night that he had climbed through the library window to call upon Agatha. It was Briscombe who had caught me peeping on the balcony and had knocked me out. Rakowitz was hanging about because he had driven Benedetto

114

over to Astor Street in his car and was waiting for him there.

It was likewise Briscombe who had burgled Dan Murphy's little shop and his flimsy shack, for he had learned that Dan collected bottles and suspected that that was what had become of the missing tonic bottle, since the police had not produced it as evidence and seemed to be accepting the theory that the poisoner had slipped the fatal drug into the medicine glass after it had been poured from the bottle.

When Juliano, from the driver's seat of the car, overheard Benedetto make that date with Jerry after the funeral, he was almost certain that Ben was going to give the show away. Just what Benedetto was really planning to say to Jerry, we shall never know. It was doubtful that he would have spoiled such a fine opportunity for blackmail which might have supported him in comfort for the rest of his life. However, Juliano could take no chances. He was desperate now.

He escorted Violet to the movies for the sake of an alibi, was careful to speak to the ticket seller as they went in so that she could vouch for their attendance together if necessary. He slid out a rear fire exit and told Violet to slip out quietly and go straight home and not tell anyone that he had not been with her all the time. She agreed to do this, having no notion what he was up to.

Juliano climbed the fire escape of the Surf Street apartment, entered the building through Valerie Burke's open window as we had figured, picked up the breadknife from the open drawer in her kitchenette and then slipped down to the next floor to wait for Ben.

Luck was with him. The corridor was deserted when Benedetto stepped nonchalantly from the elevator. One swift, skillful thrust and it was all over. The body tumbled back into the open elevator in a crumpled heap and that gave Juliano the brilliant inspiration of hiding the body there to give himself time for a getaway. Even though the elevator light was turned off, one could see into the car by the corridor lights if it were at the floor level. But if it stopped between floors so that one could not see in and if the connection were broken so that it wouldn't respond to a ring, it would be some time before the dead man was discovered. For a skilled electrician and mechanic this was not difficult to work out. He then fled down the hall, out to the fire escape again and home.

He returned to the Astor Street house a good half hour before Daggett turned up to question him and had Violet well coached. She did not get the import of his insistence on her saying he had been with her all evening until the end of the interview, and then did not have the courage to contradict herself. Even with the protection of the police, she could not bring herself to defy Briscombe. He had told her that he would kill her if she gave him away, and when she realized that his hands were already bloody, she found this threat even more terrifying.

However, when the police had gone, she accused him of murdering Benedetto and he carried her upstairs and locked her in her room. There was a stubborn streak in the little girl, however, and even though she was both awed and scared to death in Briscombe's presence, she wasn't going to be locked up like a child.

As a Britisher, she was in the habit of making herself a cup of tea in her room on an alcohol lamp when she had time in the afternoon, and she had carried a bottle of cream up to her room for her tea. That gave her the idea of the note to the milkman. She'd stuck notes in milk bottles before when Mrs. Bruns had wanted a special order. She scribbled off her note and dropped the cream bottle from the window.

The rest of the story you know already.

CHAPTER 17

SATURDAY afternoon as I was just about to leave the office, I had a call from Jerry. I had not seen him since we had left the Crane house on that awful Friday morning. I had been busy every minute since, for the newspaper office was wallowing in the biggest story for years.

"I'm over at the Astor Street house, Jim," said Jerry. "Agatha left this morning and I'm closing the place up. I'm going South for a rest the first of the week and I want to see you before I go. Can you come over to Astor Street now?"

I said I could. Virtue, looking worn and haggard, let me in. I noticed that the gilt chairs of the drawing room were already shrouded in linen covers.

"Well, Virtue," I said, "I hear that the house is being closed. What are you going to do?"

"I have a married daughter in Cleveland. I'm going on to stay with her for a bit. I shall be glad to get away. You'll find Mr. Paige in the library, sir."

There were two people sitting in the library, their chairs drawn up before a glowing fire. Jerry's russet head and Celia Emory's silvery fair one were shining close together in the firelight as I entered the room. They were bending over a box placed on a low table between them on the hearth. The dancing firelight was reflected in glinting points of colored light from this object and I realized that Jerry was showing Celia the famous Crane jewel collection which Daggett and I had checked over so hurriedly last Wednesday morning. Celia Emory will never again yearn unavailingly for jewels to hang about her lovely throat, I thought as I moved toward the absorbed pair.

Jerry sprang to his feet when he saw me. "Jim, old fellow, I'm so glad you came. I wanted to tell you before anyone else. Celia is going to marry me."

"I'm surprised and pleased, but more pleased than surprised," I grinned at them. "I wish you all sorts of happiness. You deserve a

116

little peace and joy after this past week."

"Thanks," sighed Jerry, and Celia favored me with one of her sweet, weary smiles. "You know, it's funny. We've been through so much in this awful week that it seems to both of us as if we had known each other for ages and as if some cruel fate had been keeping us apart and preventing our seeing each other, while really we never laid eyes on each other until last Tuesday night and this is only Saturday. It is silly, but we both feel that way; we were just talking about it."

"Love at first sight," I said. I always feel silly in these tender situations, but it didn't matter much what I said in this case.

"Yes, indeed it was," agreed Jerry and an ecstatic look passed between him and Celia. "But if it hadn't been for you, we might have had to spend the honeymoon in jail instead of Palm Beach. We're going to get married as soon as possible and go South for a vacation. I'm closing up the house now but will sell it later. Celia and I don't want to live here. I wish you'd take something as a remembrance. I'd like you to have a gift from Uncle Jonathan."

I remembered having noticed a beautifully bound limited edition of the works of Lawrence Sterne on the shelves.

"I might take the Montebruzzi emerald," I suggested, as I went to look for the Sterne volumes.

"Daggett brought it back from police headquarters this morning, but I shan't keep it. Celia will never wear it again and I'm not like Uncle Jonathan. My wife is going to wear those jewels."

"Well, I guess I'd rather have these books anyway," I said pulling out two handsome tooled leather volumes.

Just then there was a ring at the door. "Who is it, Virtue?" called Jerry.

"It seems to be a young man to see Miss Violet, sir," responded Virtue. "Shall I tell him to go around to the back?"

"Oh, never mind," said Jerry. "Let Violet see him in the drawing room. This is the last day."

"Very well," said Virtue.

From sheer curiosity I peered out into the hall to see who Violet's visitor was and there, perfectly recognizable in spite of the store suit and the derby hat, was my friend the milkman, Emil Holtzwarth. I popped out into the hall to greet him.

"Oh, how do you do, Mr. McBride," grinned Emil, shifting the long green florist's box he carried to his other arm, so that he could shake hands properly. "You told me it would be all right for me to meet Miss Violet, after I delivered her note and all, so I just came to call myself."

"Sure," I said heartily.

Violet came creeping down the stairs. She was still pale but looking sweet with her hair soft and smooth about her little oval face and her hazel eyes demure but bright. She smiled at me and a shadow crossed her face as she remembered what had happened when last we met. Then she glanced questioningly at the milkman who was staring at her in pleased admiration.

"Violet," I said gently, "this is the man who found your message in the cream bottle at dawn yesterday morning and took time and trouble and telephone slugs to find me and tell me about it, and he wished to meet the young lady he helped. Mr. Holtzwarth, Miss Handsley."

A faint color rose in Violet's cheeks and she looked with sweet confusion upon Emil whose wide, amiable mouth was stretched in an embarrassed grin.

"I have been wanting to meet you because it was sort of romantic, my finding your note and all and I brought you some flowers because I thought maybe it was kind of gloomy here after all that happened."

"Oh, thank you," breathed Violet, peeping at the roses in the box. "W-will you come to the kitchen with me while I put them in water?" He followed her rapturously down the hall.

I was suddenly very tired. My work at the Crane house was satisfactorily completed; no one needed me any more. I tucked my books under my arm and let myself out into the November dusk, and thought happily of a long peaceful Sunday in Oak Park, reading *Tristram Shandy* in a dressing gown and slippers.

THE END